Darkness Has Broken

Marcio Goncalves

Published by Marcio Goncalves, 2022.

DARKNESS HAS BROKEN

First edition. January 10, 2022.

Copyright © 2022 Marcio Goncalves.

ISBN: 978-0620984263

Written by Marcio Goncalves.

Table of Contents

This one goes out to all the parents who didn't get a chance to meet the children they loved.

- All characters and situations are a product of the author's imagination.

- First and foremost, all thanks, praise, honour and glory goes to Jesus Christ who makes all things possible.

- A very special thanks to Reverend Deacon Des, who so graciously accepted to read my book and write a foreword for it.

- A big thank you to Maxine Ferreira who is an incredible artist, and helped bring the rough vision of what I had in mind for the cover to life with her artistic flair and imagination.

- Thank you so much to my good friend Christina van der Merwe, an extremely talented writer and author, who so graciously edited my book.

- Lastly but certainly not least, I acknowledge YOU. Thank you for purchasing this book, and I hope you enjoy reading it as much as I enjoyed writing it, and may it bless you in whatever way the Lord deems it to touch your heart.

Darkness Has Broken

By
Marcio Goncalves

ISBN: 978-0-620-98231-3
Ebook version.
Text copyright © 2022
Marcio Goncalves
All rights reserved.
English edition

Cover was created by Maxine Ferreira, her work can be found here:
https://maxineferreira.wixsite.com/artbymaxineferreira
Edited by freelance writer and author Christina van der Merwe, her work can be found here:
https://www.upwork.com/nx/find-work/best-matches
https://www.linkedin.com/notifications/

This one goes out to all the parents who didn't get a chance to meet the children they loved.

Acknowledgements.

All characters and situations are a product of the author's imagination.

- First and foremost, all thanks, praise, honour and glory goes to Jesus Christ who makes all things possible.

- A very special thanks to Reverend Deacon Des, who so graciously accepted to read my book and write a foreword for it.

- A big thank you to Maxine Ferreira who is an incredible artist, and helped bring the rough vision of what I had in mind for the cover to life with her artistic flair and imagination.

- Thank you so much to my good friend Christina van der Merwe, an extremely talented writer and author, who so graciously edited my book.

- Lastly but certainly not least, I acknowledge YOU. Thank you for purchasing this book, and I hope you enjoy reading it as much as I enjoyed writing it, and may it bless you in whatever way the Lord deems it to touch your heart.

Foreword

I am an ordained permanent deacon at Our Lady of Perpetual Help Parish in Durbanville and have been there for almost 10 years. I have come to know Marcio over this time and have always been impressed with his diligence, work ethic, willingness to help, and his ability to rise to any challenge that he faces in his ministry or any other endeavour. I am currently mentoring him in his theological studies. Darkness Has Broken is a wonderful book in which the main character Gideon goes through many of the trials, tribulations, disappointments and emotions that affect each and every one of us during our lifetime, and then his journey from this darkness to a place of light.

The book although fiction is written with such honesty and openness; I believe this book will be a great help and comfort to anyone going through or who have gone through turbulent times in their life, knowing that there is hope, that there is light at the end of the tunnel and that our Lord Jesus will never desert us. However, the book also makes it clear that we need to open the door to allow Jesus to come into our lives, and that we cannot just sit back and wait, we need to take the steps needed to make the change.

Reverend Deacon Des Eyden.

FROM DARKNESS

"See the darkness is leaking from the cracks, I cannot contain it. I cannot contain my life."-Sylvia Plath. Three Women.

Chapter One

Mark Twain once famously said that the two most important days in a person's life, was the day they were born and the day they found out why. I would like to add to his thoughts by saying for those of us who never found out why we were born, the second most important day in our lives is the day we die. I say this because that is the day the search ends; no more anxiety, no more disappointments, no more meaningless walks through random places while contemplating oblivion, no more endless hours of staring at photographs of the past to try and figure out when exactly did life take a detour? By that line of thought, I could say that today was going to be the second most important day of my life, because by the end of this chapter, I will be dead.

I've been planning my suicide for a while, imagining the scene like a movie in great detail right down to the funeral service in the Durbanville Catholic Church. I hope by then, they would've fixed the leaky roof and noisy fans. I didn't care much for the hymns, they could choose whichever ones they wanted to use. All I wanted was for them to play that incredible monologue by Lester Burnham from my all-time favourite movie American Beauty. That to me is the most beautiful piece of cinematic art ever created. That monologue captured so perfectly the simultaneous simplicity and complexity of a human life... of *this* human's life. The sadness and obscurity of being a thirty-something year old admin clerk for a chemicals company called Stain Solutions, who lives in a bachelor flat in Durbanville town centre with no one for company but his beloved cat Hercules and about 500 books, most half-read and gathering dust in boxes. That monologue captured so precisely the symbiosis of dashed dreams, failed life goals and missed opportunities of a rapidly approaching middle-aged man who just desperately wished he could start over. That monologue captured so accurately the prison that is depression and anxiety, where I'd been incarcerated since the age of 14... and yet, there had been moments when I would look out of the tiny window of this dark state of mind and notice the beautiful blue sky or breath-taking crimson sunset. Sorry if I'm sounding a little crazy...But that doesn't bother me anymore. Lester knows what I mean. I often thought about who would come to my funeral, probably everyone except my ex-wife Lillian, which is really ironic because she was one of the biggest influences on the decision I made this morning.

Suicide has always been a silent companion in my life, kind of like the emergency exit of a bus or an aeroplane, always within reach if I noticed that the trajectory of my journey was headed for a disastrous and explosive failure, I could just pull that lever and take a more graceful exit from the grand stage of life. No one really wants to use it, but it brings everyone comfort to know that it's there in case things go beyond what we can handle. I've given up on life, because life gave up on me a very long time ago, kind of like Lillian who gave up on me too. I know she was hurting too because of what had happened to us, but she had no right to just leave without even giving me a decent explanation. Had I meant anything to her at all? I needed closure dammit! And if she wasn't going to give it to me, then I would have to make my own closure. But before I washed down my vast buffet of pills with the bottle of 12 year old Chivas Regal whisky I had bought for this special occasion, there was something I needed to do. I gave the bottle one last look, running my fingers over the label, noticing the value of the liquid gold that just got better with time, not a feeling I could relate to...

I've listened to enough rock music to know that no suicide is truly complete without a proper suicide note. So before I begin my grand exit from earth, one pill at a time, let me just grab a pen and a paper:

17 May 2018

Dear Lillian,

I know it's been ten years, but guess what?

While you've been out there living your best life, I've been here, dying in the debris of the shattered life you and I once shared. I know you don't give a damn, because if you did, you wouldn't have traded me for your boss in the first place. But at this point I don't give a damn whether you give a damn or not, think of this as the credits that roll after the movie ends, whether you ignore them or not, you cannot change the truth of what they contain.

To this day I ask myself how we went from being so in love that we would lie down together and synchronize our breathing, so that I would breathe in your air and you would breathe in mine, to barely exchanging two words in the weeks before you just walked out on me? Apart from having you rip out my heart and tear it to shreds, one of my biggest regrets is the amount of precious time I wasted on you. But anyway, what's done is done, we can't turn back time unfortunately. This isn't a letter of accusation, I'm not angry anymore, just apathetically saying goodbye because by the time you read this I will be long gone, and you won't see or hear from me ever again. I've finally made peace with the fact that despite loving you and giving you all of who I was, it wasn't good enough for you and you replaced me like dirty laundry.

I'm sorry I wasn't good enough for you, and I'm sorry that I was so wrapped up in my own grief of losing Gillian that I didn't give you any kind of support. I know that you were the one who carried her inside your womb and were obviously hurting too. I also know that we all handle our pain in different ways, unfortunately the way you chose to handle your pain, made mine a hundred times worse. But whatever, it doesn't matter now. It's done. You're happy now. Despite what you might think, I do wish you the very best, having become intimately acquainted with misery, it's not something I wish on anyone, not even the people who threw me into its abyss.

I promise to tell Gillian how much you love her, if God allows me to see her before he sends me to hell.

Part of me will be forever yours sincerely,

Gideon.

xox

Just like people who cut themselves to release their pain and watch it flow out of their skin like some kind of twisted bloodletting ritual, this suicide note to me was like making an incision on my soul and allowing it to bleed. I felt more relieved and finally ready to leave. I breathed a sigh of relief and grabbed the bottle of 12 year old Chivas Regal whisky from the coffee table and drank my way out of this world, one pill at a time. Hercules could sense something was wrong because he jumped on my lap, and pressed his head up against my belly, purring and meowing. I pet him gently, running my fingers through his soft black and white fur, it was so warm but still not quite enough to warm my cold dead heart. Hercules looked up at me with his big emerald green eyes and I couldn't help but cry because it reminded me of how I felt when Lillian had left. I finished all the pills and with one final sip, finished the bottle of whisky. Minutes later, I could feel my breathing become shallow and slowly I could feel myself sinking into a deep ocean of confusion. My thoughts were muddled and I floated in and out of consciousness, I realized that I hadn't said goodbye to my Mother, so I reached out for my mobile phone on the other side of the bed, and despite my blurred vision, I still managed to search through my contact list until I got to her name and dialled the number.

Ring....Ring...

"Mom..." I said, "Just calling to say thank you... and I love you..."

I stumbled to the nearest mirror and looked at my own reflection for one last time. My messy brown hair was all over the place, much like my life. The grey in my beard was overtaking my stubble-covered face just like the angst of failure and regret had taken over my life. My brown eyes appeared darker than I ever remember them being before, everything faded to black and the last thing I heard was the sound of my own body crashing onto the cold white tiles of my bathroom floor.

Chapter Two

"He's going into cardiac arrest... Quick, call ahead to the O.R.!" That was the voice I heard in the distance. I'm not sure where I was, but it felt like I was underwater. I could feel my entire body tingling from head to toe and yet I couldn't move. There were bursts of light flashing before my eyes and while I wasn't in unbearable pain, there was this awkward sensation in my chest that convinced me I was dying... And nothing made me happier in that moment. Suddenly, it felt like my body was plunged into a pool of icy cold water.

"We're losing him... prepare the defibrillator!"

From being ice cold to feeling like I was thrown into a pit of fire, my whole body went hot and suddenly I felt this immense pull, like my soul was leaving my body. The voices of the panicking doctors and nurses who were no doubt fighting to save my life, started to fade into the distance as I floated into a vacuum of air. I looked down and could see the medical team in a state of panic, fiddling with all the contraptions my body was connected to as they tried to save my life. But my fate was sealed with the monotonous beep of the heart monitor. I was dead, and as I continued to float out of the reality of human life, it dawned on me that I was free but now needed to prepare for hell... and that scared me more than anything else in my life. I closed my eyes as I all of a sudden fell out of the vacuum of air and landed on this patch of the greenest grass I had ever seen in my life, the sensations of the grass tickling my hands made me want to just lie there on my back forever.

I was obviously dead, right? I had seen my body just moments ago on that hospital bed, but I had never felt more alive. I stood up and started walking in no particular direction, I looked around me and all I could see was an endless stretch of this beautiful grass, I looked up at the sky and I couldn't see any birds, despite hearing them chirping in the distance. A light breeze picked up and it had this incredible scent that reminded me of the incense the priest used to burn in the church at various times of the year. I started following this scent to get to its source. The more I walked, the stronger it got, such a beautiful fragrance that filled my entire being with this incredible warmth. I noticed a bunch of trees to my right and walked towards them guessing that this inexplicable fragrance was coming from that direction. I walked in between the trees, stretched out my hands and ran my fingers through the leaves, it almost sounded like they whispered to me as they tickled my palms.

Beyond the trees, I continued to follow the mysterious fragrance, and this led me to a long staircase, so long that I couldn't see where it led to. The staircase was made of stone, and since I was no longer weighed down by a physical body, I climbed those stairs effortlessly. Everything stimulated my senses like nothing I had ever experienced before, either side of the staircase was lined with the most enchanting flowers I had ever seen, the colours were so bright and vivid it looked like the petals were alive. I stopped to smell one of them, to see if that was where the fragrance was coming from, but the fragrance was not coming from the flowers. I kept walking and to my surprise, wasn't exhausted or out of breath at all, I had none of the aches and pains that would normally plague my body after a short and brisk walk. This was great! If only I could go back to earth with this level of fitness... I would win the Olympics!

WHEN I GOT TO THE TOP of the staircase, there was an enormous white gate before me, I looked over my shoulder and could no longer see the endless stretch of garden and the trees that I had walked through. Behind me now all I could see was the sky, like a blanket of blue beneath me. I had heard many stories about the "pearly gates." But now that I was standing before them, none of what I had heard did the majestic scene of the entrance to heaven justice. The gates were white, but it sparkled with gold and had a huge sign above it that read: HOLY CITY in golden letters.

"Is this heaven?" I said to myself, "surely I don't belong here?"

The gate was left ajar, and with that incredible fragrance still filling my being with every breath, I stepped through the gap. I blinked a few times to make sure my eyes weren't deceiving me; the boundary walls adjoining the gate were made of gold, this HOLY CITY stretched as far as my eyes could see. There weren't any roads, instead there were walkways to every structure within the city, all built in gold and not a car in sight. I had heard the expression "out of this world" many times to describe various marvels of human design, but the architectural excellence I saw before me was truly out of the world I knew; I was standing at the entrance of a metropolis of the highest order, and at the expense of nothing. There was no pollution, the air was so clean it nourished my spirit. No cars, no factories, no wind turbines, nothing that could result in convenience at the expense of something else. From nature to modernized urbanization, everything was in perfect balance, just the way I imagined God intended it to be when he created it all. I looked up and saw a mountain that stretched from one side of the horizon to the other, atop of that mountain was a temple that was built all across it's summit; from within it, a light brighter than the sun shone and covered the entire city, but yet it didn't hurt my eyes. The rays of light radiating from the temple touched every single house and building in the city, every structure seemed to be drawing everything it needed to function from this power source on the mountain.

"Shalom Gideon," a voice so powerful it filled the air called out to me, but yet so gentle it put me at ease instead of fill me with fear. "Welcome to the HOLY CITY."

"Hello," I shouted, "What am I doing here?"

"All in due time," The voice boomed, but still so soothing. "Keep following the fragrance and the promptings in your heart." It reminded me of when I was a boy and my father would tuck me into bed and sing me lullabies until I fell asleep. I could listen to this mystery voice forever.

"Am I going to stay here? Where are you?" There was no response. I kept on walking following the fragrance as He had asked. When I got a little closer to the walkways, I could hear voices of people in the distance, the moment I set foot on the walkway a person appeared in front of me. I could tell he was a very athletic angel, apart from the two large wings protruding from his back, his muscular frame was three times bigger than mine.

"Shalom Gideon," He said with a smile and stretched out his enormous hand.

"Hello," I said, taking his hand that so dwarfed my own. "Sorry, I'm not Jewish, so I don't speak Hebrew."

"That's ok," he laughed, he had long blonde hair that shone like the gold around us. "Shalom means peace, we all speak from our hearts, which only knows one language here... love."

"And you are?" I couldn't resist.

"Gabriel." He sat on a rock beside the walkway that I could've sworn was not there a moment ago.

"So you were the one who told Mary about Jesus right?"

"Yes," he responded with a smile. "I'm an angel of the Lord, our task is to do our utmost to look after Abba's children on earth, whether they are aware of us or not. But I am also a messenger angel, and one of my specific tasks is to make announcements to those whom Abba wants to instruct directly. Like Mother Mary."

"Why am I here?" I asked. "Not that I'm complaining, this place is amazing, but considering how I got here, do I belong here?"

"Only Abba knows what plans he has for you," Angel Gabriel responded, "but I have been sent to give this specific message to you: it's time to let go of it all, so that you are free to receive everything Abba has been longing to give you, if you choose to accept of course." He put his hands on my shoulders, smiled and flew away, moments later, his enormous body faded into the distance of the bright blue sky.

It felt like I was in a dream, but my spirit was ignited with the kind of life that I always sought on earth but never found, I continued on the walkway, passing many beautiful houses all built in gold like the rest of the city; I looked through some of the windows and saw many happy families; some were baking bread together, others were cooking, some were playing games together, some playing with children in their gardens, others were tending to their vineyards together. But the common characteristic between them all was their smiles, their smiles radiated something I don't think I ever found with anyone except my immediate family... connection. They had this peaceful joy about them, like there was nothing more they wanted, whatever it was they were doing, their faces expressed the fulfilment of people who were doing exactly what they wanted with their lives, and lacked nothing, a concept that was totally foreign to me.

The sound of music snapped me out of the distracted state I was in, watching the families in their houses, it was coming from a building at the end of the walkway, and I just couldn't resist. I jogged there and saw that it was a pub, the doors were open and the music wasn't overwhelmingly loud, but loud enough to attract people who were longing to enjoy a drink and some good music. I walked in and noticed that the seating area was full of people, everyone was extremely friendly, they could see I was new in town and welcomed me with handshakes, hugs, big smiles and the native greeting, "shalom." Something I had to get accustomed to saying to everyone by the looks of it, if I was going to be here permanently. There was a young lady up on the stage, she must have been about twenty-two years old, she had a guitar in her hand and was singing this amazing song, her voice was so beautiful that if I was in my earthly body, it would've given me goosebumps. I just stood there in complete awe, watching her lips move as she sang a praise song to God, whom she referred to as "Abba Father."

"You always did have a weakness for women with beautiful voices Gideon," A lady appeared next to me, she had long curly black hair and a smile that reminded me so much of my mothers.

"And you are? I was puzzled and a little intrigued.

"Natalie," she replied, "I'm your sister."

"No way!" I couldn't believe it, my sister had died two years before I was born, she was born premature and unfortunately didn't make it, my mother would always cry when she spoke of her. If only she knew that my sister had inherited her smile. "But you died as a baby, and here you're all grown up? How is that even possible?"

"When Abba assigned me to pray for you, He allowed me to grow with you throughout your life," she said, "I guess it was in preparation for this moment. Abba knows all things brother. Oh how I prayed for you..." She had tears in her eyes and gave me the tightest hug I had ever gotten from anybody in my life, it felt so welcoming. I didn't want her to let go.

"Why does everyone call God, Abba here?" I asked. "To me Abba is that awful band mom and dad used to play on their radio at full volume on weekends."

"I think Abba are great by the way," she said laughing, "Abba means father in Hebrew, and when Abba went down to earth born as a man for our salvation, He was born Jewish, so we call Him Abba as a sign of respect and reverence."

"Would you like a drink?" Natalie asked.

"Do they have beer here?" My eyes lit up, realizing that liquidized hop and barley would be one of the very few things about earth I would miss.

"We only drink wine here," Natalie replied, signalling to the bar man for two cups. "But I promise you, the wine here is better than anything else you will ever drink."

They served the wine in clay cups, and when I put my lips to the cup and took a sip, my whole body tingled with absolute satisfaction. It was sweet to the tongue and buttery smooth, with a gentle spicy after taste that lingered. Truly the best drink I had ever had.

"Will this make me drunk?" I laughed.

"Only in the spirit like St Paul wrote," Natalie laughed.

"Do you know how many times I wondered what it would be like if you had survived and been in my life?"

"I heard you tell everyone you would've dated all my friends," she gave me that same look mom used to give me before giving me a hiding. "Is that all I would've been good for to you brother?"

"What else are sisters for?" I winked at her, and we had a good laugh after she playfully punched my arm.

"To family," I raised my cup to her, so happy that I finally knew what it felt like to have a sister.

"To family!" The whole bar raised their voices and their glasses, and everyone laughed as Natalie and I toasted.

"We're all family here," Natalie said.

"Speaking of family," I asked. "Where's dad?"

"Abba sent him on a mission,: Natalie replied hesitantly.

"What kind of mission?"

"I don't know... We don't question anyone's relationship with Abba here, He loves us all and we trust that no matter where He sends us or what He does, it's for the good of the entire city and everyone in it. That's good enough for us, no need to ask questions."

"I miss him..."

"Abba knows," she said. "Best you get going, Abba is waiting for you." She playfully pushed me away from the bar.

"Where?" I said, finishing my wine. "How will I know him?"

"When you're ready to meet him," Natalie walked with me outside. "He will come and meet you." She kissed me on the cheek and gave me a hug. "It was so good to see you brother."

"I'm so happy to have met you sis," I said.

"Go..." She smiled. "Until we meet again."

Chapter Three

Jeremiah 1:5
Before I formed you in the womb I knew you, before you were born I set
you apart; I appointed you as a prophet to the nations.

I didn't know where I was going, but so far had enjoyed the trip through the HOLY CITY; I had met an angel, seen the most incredible sights that no stretch of my imagination could've come up with, I met my sister, drank the most incredible wine that no human hands could've made and with all these experiences I was keen for the journey to continue.

With the jubilations of the pub fading behind me, I walked into what looked like a park. There were trees all around me, some bore fruit and others had these enormous branches that created shapes on the grass with their shadows. There was a water fountain in the middle of the park and a few benches, the sound of the water flowing through the fountain reminded me of the fish tank I had as a teenager, how the sound of the filter would help me fall asleep. The water was so clear that it's surface sparkled in the light. I heard a flock of birds fly overhead, they were white doves, their wings were on fire and as they glided in the sky; the warmth of their flaming wings descended onto me like dew. I looked to my right and noticed an enormous white lion approaching, I was terrified! This was it! I was certain that hell had finally arrived to get me and all that had happened was just to lure me into a false sense of spiritual security.

"Shalom Gideon," a voice spoke up from behind me, it was a man and He walked up to the lion and pet him, his white mane sparkled like glitter and he purred so loud, it echoed throughout the park. "Don't be afraid, he won't harm you."

The man's presence struck me immediately. He didn't look exactly like all the paintings done of him on earth, but the depictions weren't far off from how the world had come to portray him. He had long dark hair and a beard, his skin had the tone of someone who spent most of their days outdoors. But his eyes were what stopped time for me, I couldn't tell what colour they were because they had different shades to them, but they were as deep as the ocean and as limitless as the sky. When he looked at me, it's like his eyes pierced me right down to the soul, it's like he knew everything about me right down to my thoughts even before they occurred.

"Jesus?"

"To some Jesus, to others Yeshua, others still Rabbi, Father, Abba," He smiled and walked up to me. "What matters is that you know who I am in here," He touched my chest and it set my spirit on fire. "Welcome my son." He gave me a hug and I was so overcome with emotion that I just started to cry.

"Let's go for a walk shall we?" He wiped the tears from my eyes, like a father would to his child, and all of a sudden the guilt of not having committed my life to Him slowly began to fade.

"This place is incredible," I said, and followed him, as he led the way.

"This is home," he said, we were walking through this patch of fruit trees that had the finest looking fruit I had ever seen; lemons, apples, oranges, granadillas and mangos.

"A home for all my children should they choose it, if only they understood that it would be so much more profitable for them to store up treasures for themselves here rather than on earth where evil lurks."

The smell of fresh fruit was making me hungry for the first time since I got here, but I wasn't going to say anything, I was dead, I wasn't supposed to be hungry. We continued walking in silence, but not an awkward silence that needed to be filled, instead the silence was fulfilling, like when we are with someone we love and just enjoy each other's company for what it is, not for what we think it should be based on human standards. We were approaching a vineyard, and at the entrance Jesus picked a bunch of grapes from the vine that was hanging above our heads.

"Grapes?"

"Yes please," I replied, they were the sweetest grapes I had ever eaten in my life. So delicious I had to close my eyes to savour the taste.

"There are some people I want you to meet here," He said. I followed Him to the building adjacent to the vineyard.

"Shalom Rabbi!" Three men ran out to greet Jesus before we could reach the entrance.

"Shalom," Jesus answered hugging them, "we have a visitor."

"Ah yes, shalom Gideon." They all shook my hand and proceeded to give me a hug.

"This is Peter, James and his brother John, the sons of Zebedee," Jesus said, introducing them to me.

"Um... Shalom," I said, not knowing quite how to react to being introduced to the three men who had walked closest to Jesus when He was on earth.

"You're a fast learner," Peter said, laughing.

"Do you like it here?" James asked.

"It's incredible..." I replied, trying not to get too attached because I didn't know if I was going to stay here.

"Why don't you boys show him around, while I go attend to that business we spoke of this morning?"

"Absolutely," John said. "I will take him to you when we're done."

"Perfect," Jesus said, "see you soon Gideon." He waved at us and walked off.

"Do you know how to make wine?" They asked with the enthusiasm of children about to show off their new toys.

"I know how to drink it, and the wine here is amazing."

"Always the funny guy," they laughed.

"James, Peter," John said, "why don't you guys go and prepare for dinner, let me take care of our new friend Gideon here."

"Don't let him start telling you stories," James advised.

"You'll fall asleep," Peter said and they walked off laughing.

"Get out of here!" John laughed, and pushed them outside.

"Welcome Gideon," He said, "those two are always clowning around."

"They seem like great guys to work with," I laughed.

"We don't just work together... over here, we're family."

"My sister said the same thing," I replied.

"She was so excited to meet you, even though she was saddened by what had happened."

"I'm starting to think I should've done it sooner," I said.

"Gideon, my brother..." John said, looking at me with an expression of deep concern. "You didn't remove your pain, you just put it in the hands of those you left behind." His words hit me much harder than I thought they would, I was convinced no one loved me or would even miss me, who could he be talking about?

"I'm going to show you how we make wine... You ready?" John said, with a broad smile.

"As ready as I have ever been," I replied.

"Come on," he said.

I followed him to the store house behind the machines at the wine press. He opened the door and there were buckets and buckets full of grapes, spread across the store house floor. John grabbed two chairs from the stack behind the door of the entrance and placed them at the centre of the room.

"Could you kindly bring me two buckets please?"

"Sure," I grabbed them and returned to where he had put the chairs.

"I am sorting the grapes, to make sure only the best ones are chosen to make the wine," he said, grabbing a bunch and going through them one by one. "When our lives start, we're like any shoot off of a vine; tender, green and full of potential. Just like the quality of grapes depends on how we look after the vine, what kind of fruits our lives will bear depends largely on what decisions we make with our lives." He was tossing the grapes two by two into the crate. As a vineyard keeper, we need to make sure that the vine remains healthy by removing any bad grapes, before they attract insects with their rot that will end up feeding on the good grapes and ruin the entire vine. Our lives are the same, due to sin we will produce bad fruits in our lives, but it's important to be mindful of those fruits and remove them promptly so that the good fruits in our lives are not ruined." I was in awe at how he was using something as simplistic as making wine to teach a spiritual lesson that would have a life-long impact. Jesus had taught him well. "The problem is if we don't remove the bad grapes from the good ones," before I had even noticed the crate was already full. "They will all go into the winepress at harvest and ruin the entire batch of wine." He gave me a grape to taste, and popped one into his own mouth.

"Good grapes will make good wine. So it's so important to make sure only the good grapes get chosen to go to the winepress. So it is with us, if we produce good fruits with our lives, we will get chosen to go to where we're destined to be and produce that which is good for the kingdom of God."

John grabbed the full crate, and asked me to follow him to the wine press. He dunked the grapes from the crate and into the machine that was going to press them into juice, which would flow into a roller dish that was separating the pulp from the juice.

"The destiny of every grape is to be pressed for wine, that is why grapes were created, and the pressing hurts. But it's a necessary process for the grapes to reach their full potential," he said, watching the grapes getting pressed. "We're the same, God has picked each one of us for a purpose and if we don't fulfil our purpose then we will get tossed like the bad grapes. But God loved us so much, and didn't want any of us to be destroyed, so He voluntarily stood in our place in the person of Jesus Christ and got tossed on our behalf, so that we would have a chance to be chosen to stand with the good grapes. But that chance is up to us to take with both hands. It' not easy, it sometimes hurts, but it's worth it. We're not capable of producing good fruits on our own, but through Jesus Christ who strengthens us, we can all be good grapes." He tossed another grape in his mouth. "The choice is always ours. Everything can be taken from us except the freewill to choose how we react to whatever happens. That's a gift given to us by Abba that no one will take away from any of us."

"Thank you," I said, in awe of his practical teaching.

"Now come on," John said, "Jesus is waiting for you."

John took me to Jesus who was sitting at the top of hill at a stone table, He waved at us when He saw us approaching. The view from the top of the hill was incredible.

"I trust you are an expert at wine making by now?" He smiled at us.

"I think Gideon understood everything I told him," John winked at me. "I will leave you both to it. Shalom Gideon."

"Shalom John, thank you."

"Please take a seat," Jesus pointed at the available seat across from where He was sitting.

"Your sister told me you would love the winemaking tour," Jesus said.

"She was right," I replied, "even though I am more of a beer drinker. As you can see," I tapped my belly.

"Always up for a good laugh," Jesus said, chuckling.

"Can I ask you something?" I replied.

"I've been expecting you to ask," Jesus said.

"I'm obviously dead," I replied, "and given that I took my own life, I shouldn't be here. Not that I am complaining, but why am I here?"

"Gideon..." He said, "Stop thinking about the destination, even before taking your first step. Just enjoy the journey, one moment at a time." I looked down at the stone table between us and noticed that my name was engraved into it with a timeline starting at the date of my conception. "Spending your time making others laugh, has done little or nothing to remove your own pain," He said, and reached out to grab my hand. "There's no need to defend yourself here Gideon... Are you ready to take my hand and allow me to heal you? Allow me to press you, so you can be transformed?"

"Yes," I took a deep breath and felt us both go into a vacuum of air, through it all I didn't let go of His Hand.

There was a flash of light before my eyes, and I saw an unborn baby growing in a young woman's womb. She had green eyes and dark her, but it was her unmistakable smile that made me recognize that this woman was my mother when she was pregnant with me. She was sitting at her bedroom window, watching the rain outside. Jesus and I were in the room with her, but as mere spectators, watching this memory of my mother's life and mine. She was rubbing her belly, a look of pain and anxiety on her face.

"I lost your sister," she whispered, "there's no way I am going to lose you."

A car pulled up the driveway of the two bedroom house in Johannesburg, where I was born. It was my dad, I recognized him immediately, with his thick black hair, Elvis Presley sideburns, he had no greys but his confident gait was unmistakable.

"Maria," he said, walking into the bedroom and greeting my mom with a kiss. "Are you ready to go?"

"You can close your eyes for those scenes Gideon," Jesus laughed, noticing how awkward it was for me to see my parents kissing while pregnant with me.

"Thank you." I laughed.

They got into the car and rushed off to the hospital, the nurses were already waiting with a wheelchair and my dad went straight to the doctor ahead of my mom as they nurses pushed her gently to his office.

"Mr and Mrs Daniels," the Doctor said after doing a scan. "Unfortunately history has repeated itself, and your womb is not going to hold this baby full tern, I am going to admit you immediately to try and prolong the pregnancy, at this stage every day counts. We don't want you to lose another child."

"What?" My dad said, "At seven months, will our boy survive?"

"We going to do the best we can, and hope for the best," he said. "Now if you excuse me, I need to prepare her bed in the ward."

"Doctor," My mother grabbed the doctor's arm, and she was crying. "Please save my baby..."

"Mrs Daniels," he grabbed her hand. "You have my word that I am going to do everything in my power to make sure your child is ok."

The worry on my mom's face and the tears rolling down her cheeks just broke my heart, and I started crying with her. Suddenly I started thinking about all the times I mistreated her, the stupid arguments we had, the times I took advantage of her kindness, or the times I brushed her off as she got older, and I felt like the worst man in the world.

"He's going to be ok Maria," My dad said, reassuring her, once she was settled into the ward. "I've got to go to work, I will see you tonight."

"Dear Lord Jesus and dear Mother Mary," My mom said out loud noticing that she was alone in the ward. "If you spare my child and me, I promise that when he is old enough, on the first holiday we take together I will take him to Cova De Iria in Portugal and put a candle up in thanksgiving for granting me this miracle. Please. I don't think I can handle losing another child. Don't take this baby away from me. Please." Hot tears drenched her pale cheeks.

"Your mother Maria is a wonderful woman that I am very fond of," I granted her the miracle, and she honoured her promise." Jesus put his arm around my shoulder to comfort me. "My Mother never stopped praying for you, you know."

That promise my mother made was fulfilled when I was five years old. I didn't understand the significance of it all, nor did I appreciate the emotional impact of it all until this moment, when I actually saw it all with my own eyes. Even Mother Mary was praying for me to pull through...

"Now that you understand how many people were praying and sacrificing for you to pull through," He said, "now that I hope you see how precious you are to your mother, to me, to my mother... I want to take you through seven events in your life that fundamentally shaped who you became. Through these seven memories, just like My Father created everything in six days and rested on the seventh, I hope to take away all the old inside of you and make you a new creation, if you will allow me?"

My tears were enough of a response, no words were needed.

Chapter Four

M<u>emory 1</u>
Isaiah 43:1
Do not fear for I have redeemed you; I have summoned you by name, you are mine.

Jesus and I were standing on the steep inclined driveway of number 12 Hope Avenue, where I had grown up. I was filled with so much aching nostalgia, that it felt like I was going to burst, as I remembered the hot summer days of my childhood spent bowling my cricket ball at the fig tree my dad planted in our garden. Back then all I dreamed about was being a cricket player, I would day dream about playing alongside the greats like Alan Donald, Shaun Pollock, Jonty Rhodes and Lance Klusener.

"You must be wondering why we're here," Jesus said, pointing at the red gate which led to the entrance of the house opposite the garage.

"I was too busy reliving my childhood," I replied, "but yes, I am curious."

"All my children on earth spend their entire childhood wanting to grow up, then spend their whole adult lives trying to relive what they lost as children. It doesn't have to be that way Gideon. Life is given to all of you, one moment at a time. That is the best way to live it, holding onto my hand as I guide your steps one day at a time."

"The world was a scary place for me Lord," I replied.

"Everything that grows starts as a seed, and then gathers root," Jesus replied. "I want to show you how the seed of your fears and anxieties that you carried your entire life got planted and took root inside of you, so that we can pull it out... together. Are you ready?"

"Yes Lord," I replied, hesitantly but knowing that somehow, someway I would make it through if he was with me.

Jesus waved his hand, and then we were standing inside the house as eye witnesses to this particular memory from my childhood. Eight year old me was sitting on the floor in front of the TV, watching Tom and Jerry, when my mother's voice came thundering through the house.

"Gideon!" She shouted, "I need tomatoes, please go to Rita's and buy some for me!"

Rita was the owner of the café at the end of our street. I obeyed her but moaned and groaned all the way there because I was missing my favourite cartoon. Rita was a friendly old lady, and looked like everyone's favourite aunt; hair white as wool, glasses at the tip of her nose and permanent red cheeks with a warm smile that welcomed everyone who walked into her shop.

"Hello Gideon!" Rita said, immediately leaving her cash register to come and give me a big hug. "How's mom, young man?"

"She's fine," I said, grabbing the packet of tomatoes and wanting to pay so I could get back to my cartoons.

"Send her my regards," Rita said, ruffling my hair and she put a chocolate in my hand.

"Thank you so much Aunty Rita," I waved at her before walking out.

The free chocolate made it worth losing my favourite cartoon, I unwrapped it and started savouring the sweetness, one bite at a time. I was so busy enjoying my chocolate I didn't notice that the gate of number 7 Hope Avenue was open, until their dog was chasing me down the street.

"Aah!"

I don't think I've ever ran so fast in my entire life, I could hear the dogs jaws snapping at my heels, this forced me to give an extra push and my mind was totally focused on the entrance gate of my house. I put one hand on the gate and launched myself over it, eventually landing on my back after scraping my arms and legs on the way down. I could feel the dogs breath on my face as he snarled at me from beyond the gate a few times before turning around and walking off. I took a deep breath, felt the adrenaline subside, and felt the sting of my cuts and scrapes. The whole episode came back to me in flashbacks as I closed my eyes and cried, I lost whatever was left of my chocolate, but I had the tomatoes my mom needed.

"Gideon?" My mom must've heard my cries, "are you alright?" She rushed to my side.

"Sorry mom," I replied, "one of the neighbour's dogs chased me and I thought I was going to die."

"Oh no," she held me. "It's ok, you're safe now." I could still hear the dogs jaws snapping at my heels, I had nightmares for a week. But my mom never sent me to Rita's Café alone ever again after that.

"You suffered with anxiety your whole life," Jesus said, turning to me. "This event was the seed that planted the fear and anxiety in your spirit, psychologically you had an irrational fear of dogs and that fear became the foundation upon which every other crippling burden you ever had was built upon."

"Really?" I had almost forgotten this memory, but was so touched by the care and detail Jesus put in to helping me cast my burdens on him.

"Fear is one of the enemy's most effective tools against my children," Jesus replied. "He kept you captive on a subconscious level, using the seed of fear he planted on the day you were chased by that dog."

"So how are we going to remove it?" I asked.

"Gideon, do you remember the story of how I stopped the storm for my disciples when they saw me walk on water?"

"Yes I remember hearing that many times," I replied.

"You know the centre of a storm is always calm, the eye of the storm is completely peaceful. The storm is only chaotic on the outside. That day with my disciples, I made it possible for them to see me, at the centre of the storm, to encourage them to face the storm head on while keeping their eyes on me in order that I could guide them through it." He smiled. "For this particular memory of yours, I am going to do the same thing, I am going to put you back there and make you face the fear, but this time I want you to call on me, so I can see you through the storm of your fear, guide your steps and bring you into my peace at the eye of it."

"You want me to face the dog?" I was puzzled, how are you going to fit the adult me into my childhood body?"

"Gideon," Jesus said gently, "don't overthink things, one moment at a time, and never forget how much I love you..."

Seconds later, I was inside my eight year old body. I couldn't change anything about the sequence of events, I was like a spectator to the memory but from inside my own body.

"Jesus.. Jesus," I said, "what do you want me to do?"

"Exactly what you're doing now," He replied, "call on me when you're feeling overwhelmed."

Going through the entire memory again, as Aunty Rita ruffled my hair, I wondered if she was in heaven, and Jesus interrupted my thoughts.

"Yes she is Gideon," He said. "I've put her in charge of the children's home here in heaven. She never had children of her own, so I gave her all the babies who were rejected by their parents on earth, the aborted and abandoned babies. She's a special daughter of mine, with a heart that's big enough to love all those babies that were unwanted."

Something changed as I reached the part of my memory where eight year old me was passing the front gate of number 7 Hope Avenue. It' like I had returned completely to that day, I could feel my entire body again, every sensation, but still couldn't control the sequence of events. It's like I was there in body and mind, but not in spirit. I was literally reliving the moment, and as the dog started barking and I could hear his jaws snapping at my heels; my mind went into the same frenzy as it did the first time around, and as the adrenaline started rushing through my veins, I was suddenly mindful of what Jesus had said:

"Jesus!" I shouted, "Jesus help me!"

The sequence of events hadn't changed, the dog still chased me and I still ran for my life, but I had this inexplicable calm about me, I could no longer hear the dog's jaws snapping at my heels, my heart was beating but not out of fear, more due to extreme focus on getting to my gate. It' like I had this peace because I knew I was going to make it, and that gave me strength and kept me calm. When I got to the gate, I put my hand on it and launched myself over it. This time, because I was more calm, although I fell hard, I didn't hurt myself as badly. I watched the dog snarling at me, but it didn't scare me at all. It's like I had a shield over my mind and heart. I had no fear, the fear was gone.

"Gideon," I heard Jesus's voice calling me and pulling me out of the memory. Once again we were seated at the stone table with the timeline of my life engraved on it. "When soldiers go out for battle, they never leave without putting on their armour. I have prepared spiritual armour for all my children to put on every day before they go out onto the battlefield of life."

"Where do I find this armour Lord?" I asked.

"Here," He raised His Hand, and a bright light shone through it, and a Bible appeared on the palm of His Hand. He laid it on the table, paged through it and asked me to read it:

Ephesians 6:10-18
Finally my brethren, be strong in the Lord and in His Mighty power put on the full armour of the God, that you may be able to stand against the

wiles of the devil. For we do not wrestle against flesh and blood, but against principalities, against powers, against the rulers of darkness of this age, against spiritual hosts of wickedness in heavenly places. Therefore take up the whole armour of God, that you may be able to stand, stand therefore having girded your waist with truth, having put on the breastplate of righteousness, and having shod your feet with the preparation for the gospel of peace; above all taking the shield of faith with which you will be able to quench all the fiery darts of the wicked one. And take the helmet of salvation, and the sword of the spirit, which is the word of God; praying always with all prayer, and supplication in the spirit, being watchful to this end with all perseverance and supplication for all the saints.

THE PAGES WERE AS WHITE as the light shining onto His Hand, and the letters were written in gold, almost as if they were on fire, the word was alive and as I read it, I could feel the fire ignite in my spirit. Only then had I noticed there was an angel by my side, dressing the armour I was reading about over me, I truly felt girded with the Lord's armour after reading that scripture.

"If only I had known," I said, looking at Jesus with the heaviness of guilt in my spirit.

"Gideon," He grabbed my hands. "No matter what happens, just take My Hand and trust Me."

"Yes Lord."

"Let's move on," He smiled and ran his finger along the timeline of my life, and engraved letters on the stone turned to fire.

Chapter Five

M<u>emory 2</u>

Acts 4:11-12

Jesus is the stone you builders rejected, which has become the cornerstone.

The flaming letters of the year 1996 went out of focus as I held onto Jesus's Hands, we went up into a vacuum of air as we travelled through the time and space continuum of my existence on earth. It lasted mere seconds, and I never loosened my grip on Jesus's Hands, looking always at His smiling face the whole time. We landed on a field.

"Remember this place Gideon?" Jesus asked

I looked around and noticed the white pavilion adjacent to the field, the rolling hills behind us and the familiar buildings on the opposite side, and of course the Holy Redeemer Catholic Church in the distance. I knew exactly where we were.

"Selly Park Primary," I whispered, recalling all the fond memories of my childhood. "You know Lord, I didn't think so at the time, but the years I spent here were the best of my life. Not all the memories were good, but I really enjoyed my time here."

"I was very pleased when your parents decided to start your education here," Jesus replied.

"Great Saint Paul, our heavenly patron..." I sang, remembering our school anthem.

For a split second, I wished I could be back here, reliving my childhood and with a chance to start my life over. But time doesn't go back, and that's one of life's greatest tragedies, once the moment is gone, it doesn't come back, and if we miss the opportunity to make the best out of each moment, then it's gone, it's wasted.

"It was there that I started to call you to something better Gideon," Jesus pointed to the church, right next to the school building. "But more about that a little later.. are you ready to see another one of the events that shaped your life?"

"Yes Lord," I replied.

Just like before, we were watching the memory as eye witnesses, I had a feeling I knew what He was going to show me, I got over it or I thought I did, but He had a plan and if He was taking me back to that time in my life, then there must have been a good reason for it. So I was going to trust Him and face whatever it was He wanted to show me. It was a hot Thursday afternoon, we had all just changed into our school sports uniforms and we were waiting for coach Du Plessis to arrive on the field to tell us what we were going to do.

"Good afternoon children," his thick moustache had always reminded me of a cactus. "Today we're going to play Rounders."

"Yay!" Everyone started cheering, because Rounders was much more fun than normal exercise, it was Coach Du Plessis's version of baseball, except we used a tennis ball and racquet.

"Melissa and Thabo," He said, "I nominate you as the team captains today, come up here and pick your teams, one at a time."

Athletic ability was never one of my strengths, and as much as it hurt to never get picked for any sporting activity that we participated in, I was used to it. I always ended up falling into one of the teams by default because I was always the last one that no one picked. I was resigned to that fact. This time, I fell into Thabo's team by default. Unsurprisingly, Melissa's team won. I was the weakest link in Thabo's team, and everyone was moaning and groaning about how they lost the game because of me. We went to the toilets to freshen up and get changed out of our sports clothes before going home.

"Hey fatty!"

I was right, Jesus was showing me the memory of when I got bullied at school. I remember how furious I was, but Thabo was bigger and stronger than me, and had friends, which I never had. So as much as I wanted to do something, I just couldn't. I was incapacitated in every way against him.

"Thabo..." I turned to face him.

"We lost because of you today," he started to pace around me, like a shark circulates its prey before launching an attack.

"I'm sorry," I replied, "I don't know why Mr Du Plessis insists I play, he knows I'm no good."

"You are no good," Thabo walked right up to me, until we were face to face. "You're no good at sports, you don't have any friends, you're fat and ugly, is there anything you're good for?" I could feel his hot breath on my face.

"At least I brush my teeth," I replied, waving my hand in front of my face.

Like many times in my life, my mouth got me into serious trouble. Thabo slapped me to the ground and kicked me a few times. He then picked me up and continued to slap and punch me, before grabbing my arm and twisting it behind my back, holding me up against the wall. "Every Thursday when we have sports, you are going to give me your lunch. Do you understand?" He twisted my arm a little more.

"Yes!" I was on the verge of tears, afraid that my arm was about to break.

"Good," he slapped my face lightly, "that way, you will be good enough for me and you'll lose some weight." He put his arm around my shoulder after loosening his grip on me. "I don't need to tell you what will happen to you if anyone hears about our little arrangement, do I?"

"No," I was fighting hard not to cry.

"Good," he laughed, and strode off like a victorious tyrant.

"I'm sorry you had to go through that," Jesus said.

"I don't know why he was so mean," I replied. "I'm glad we didn't end up in the same high school."

"Let me show you something," Jesus waved his hand and our background shifted to a completely different setting, like we were in a science-fiction movie.

We were standing in a kitchen, a woman who was dishing out the meal she had prepared onto the plates set at the table for her family. But she had a terrified look on her face, her hands were even shaking as she was heaping spoonful's of rice onto the plates.

"Lerato!" A voice thundered through the house. "Bring me a beer!"

"We're going to have dinner," Lerato responded, "can't you drink your beer with the meal?"

Moments later the man charged into the kitchen, he had a bewildered look on his face, and seemed like he had drunk one too many beers already. "Are you being disobedient again?" He shouted.

"No I was just..." He grabbed her by the hair and pulled so hard she screamed.

"I'm the only one who asks questions here," he slapped her so hard, she fell to the ground and slid across the kitchen floor. "Now bring me that beer!"

Then I saw him... Thabo crept into the kitchen, tears streaming down his face, when he saw his mother stumbling back to her feet. I couldn't believe that I was watching a scene from Thabo's house, and what he had to go through with his parent's troublesome relationship.

"Thabo sweety," his mother said, trying to compose herself. "Everything is fine, we just had a disagreement."

"Mom, did he hurt you again?"

"Your mother was being disobedient again," He grabbed Thabo by the arm and picked him up. "But of course, you're always taking her side." He slapped him and threw him to the ground, he rolled across the floor to where his mother had fallen.

"Why?" Thabo was wailing.

"I'm always the bad one!" His father spat. "That's what everyone thinks! I'm the drunk who beats his wife and kid, but what people don't know is why I do it. You're no good! Both of you are no good!"

Jesus took my hand and we were back at the stone table. I felt so sorry for Thabo, I had no idea of what he was going through at home, but now that I had seen the whole picture of his life, his behaviour made much more sense. Underneath that tough kid exterior was a wounded and scared soul.

"Man, Thabo had an awful childhood," I said.

"He lived with that well into his high school years," Jesus said. "Until his father got gravely ill and finally stopped drinking."

"How is he now?"

"I CALLED HIS FATHER home recently, but not before putting someone in his life to help him heal, repent and reconcile with his son," Jesus said. "Thabo is ok now, he was quickly following in the only footsteps his father had shown him, footsteps of anger, bitterness. However, one fine day, Thabo listened to the promptings I put in his heart, came to church and there I put a girl on his path to help him heal and through her love, he was renewed."

"I'm really happy to hear that," I said, smiling genuinely at the thought of how things had turned out for him.

"My children don't have to live according to the rejection or standards of man that keep changing" He grabbed my hands again. "I became the cornerstone that the builders rejected in your place, so that you could be free of that. Free of anger, free of rejection, free of bitterness, let go of all that breaks you down, so that you can claim the life I obtained for you in abundance Gideon. For you and for all my children..."

Chapter Six

M<u>emory 3</u>

Luke 15:6-7

Then he calls his friends and neighbours together and says, "Rejoice with me, I have found my lost sheep. I tell you that in the same way there will be more rejoicing in heaven over one sinner who repents than over ninety-nine righteous person who do not need to repent.

I was so happy to just be exactly where I was in the presence of the Lord. I can't remember having ever lived without a care in the world. There was nowhere I needed to go, no bills I had to pay. I was just sitting there enjoying life as it was given to me. Heaven was amazing. A lady arrived at our table serving bread and olives with wine.

"Shalom my child," Jesus said, smiling at her. "This is Gideon."

"Shalom Abba," She replied, "Ah yes Gideon, Abba said we might have a guest here this week. Shalom."

"Shalom," I replied, feeling a little disconcerted by her saying that I was a guest, did it mean I wasn't going to stay? Why would Jesus go through all this trouble, only to tell me to leave?

Jesus whispered something in her ear, she smiled at me and waved before walking off; her eyes sparkled like diamonds and her black hair was shining in the light. Other than Gabriel, I had never seen an angel, but I imagined them looking like that woman.

"Is she an angel?"

"No, remember that story in the Bible of the woman I saved from being stoned to death at the hand of the Pharisees?"

That's her?" I was amazed to see the actual people that I had read about and heard of in Bible class throughout my childhood.

"I remember the day well," Jesus said, looking as if He was deep in thought. "Throwing stones is so easy Gideon, it takes a much bigger effort and removal of one's selfish ambitions to put the stones down."

"Shall we eat?"

"Only if you want to," I replied.

"With a grateful heart I give thanks for this opportunity to spend time with Gideon," Jesus said, raising the olives and bread. "As we share this meal together, I declare come Holy Spirit and fill Gideon with Your Presence so that as we continue on this journey, He may be cleansed, healed, restored and transformed. Amen."

"Amen," I replied.

"Enjoy," Jesus said pushing the bread and olives to my side of the table so I could help myself.

"Thank you." The olives were incredible, and complimented the buttery after taste of the wine to perfection.

"This next memory," Jesus now helped himself to the food. "is something that most of my children struggled with, once you're done, we'll get going."

We had finished our meal, and once more Jesus grabbed my hand and we went through the time and space continuum of my life. The place we arrived at sent a wave of discomfort through me, I could feel it rise up from the pit of my stomach like a wound.

"Remember when I told you that the rejection you experienced in your childhood became the foundation upon which the rest of your life's burdens were built?"

"Yes?"

"Well what happened in this house, was a proof of what I mean when I said that."

We were standing at the front door of the house I used to share with my ex-wife Lillian. I swore I would never return, and being here now even though I was dead, didn't feel very good:

Lillian had left the lights on, but the minute I walked through the front door and noticed that the TV was off, I knew something was amiss. I remember my heart beating really fast as I walked through the house, calling out to her. I walked through every bedroom, she was nowhere to be found, but it wasn't until I opened her wardrobe and noticed that all her clothes were gone that I realized Lillian was part of my past. She was gone. On my way out of the bedrooms, I noticed a note stuck to the door with a drawing pin; asking me for a divorce, listing too many explanations and excuses which boiled down to the same reason; she stopped loving me, or never did to begin with. Thabo's words echoed in my head: *"you really are good for nothing..."*

"Lord, you knew I was not well," I couldn't control myself, standing there next to Jesus in the house that was mine. The painful rejection I had experienced back then had come back and it felt like a dagger to the heart. "You knew what had happened and yet more than let her leave, you allowed her to replace me as well." My voice was getting louder, as flashbacks of the times I saw her out and about with the new man in her life; going to the places she had gone to with me, sharing the life we had planned for ourselves with him. "I remember the nights I would lie next to her in bed, but she was thousands of miles away." The anger was just pouring out of me. "You know what frustrates me the most right now... It's not that I wanted her back. What hurts the most, is that all these years later... And she's moved on with her life, and me? I was still stuck in the ruins she left me in. I felt like Samson, when he pushed those pillars apart, dead underneath the rubble of my own life. It's not that I needed her unhappiness for me to be happy," I was pacing around now, trying to process the sheer volume of emotions filtering through my words.

"But why couldn't I have moved on with my life and found someone else too? She was the one who left me! She was the one who broke the covenant we made in front of your altar, and yet, she was the one who ended up happy and I ended up so miserable I chose to end my life. Do you think that's fair!?" Out of sheer frustration I swung a fist at the window behind us with all my strength and to my shock I broke it.

"Are you finished?" He asked, looking me straight in the eyes.

"You tell me..." My face was drenched in tears. "Please?"

He wiped my face with the sleeve of His bright white tunic and just hugged me. I held onto Him like a little boy would hold his father. I didn't want to let Him go, and as I held onto Him ever so tight, I remembered the words of the prayer I learnt in religious studies class in school:

Come Holy Spirit fill the hearts of Your faithful and kindle in them the fire of Your love. Send forth Your Spirit and they shall be created. And You shall renew the face of the earth.

As Jesus held on to me, I could feel the physical manifestation of this prayer inside of me. As the Holy Spirit filled my heart, and kindled the fire of His love inside of me, the immense pain of being rejected by the one person I gave myself to completely just lifted and I felt the peace of the Holy Spirit just wash over me.

"Gideon," Jesus said and put His Hand on my shoulder. "It's time to forgive and let go."

"I've tried.." I shrugged, "but it has never worked."

"That's because you're starting in the wrong place," Jesus replied. "You have to start here first," He touched my chest. "How can you forgive anyone, if you still believe the lies the enemy has planted in your head through the pain others have caused you? Before you can forgive Lillian and everyone else, you have to forgive yourself and believe that you are good enough for someone, even if she didn't think you were good enough for her." Jesus waved his hand over the broken window, and all the pieces just came back into place until it was fully restored.

"Just like with Thabo, you also don't know what Lillian had to go through in her life before she met you, she also didn't know what you went through before meeting her." Jesus said. "She too was rejected in her youth, she was overweight, had acne and had an abusive father. By the time she met you she had blossomed into the beautiful girl I had created her to be, but her self-worth was completely gone and that's why I put you in her life. I was hoping that by the commitment the two of you had made to each other I would be able to heal you both through one another. But unfortunately she healed a lot faster than you and thanks to how you loved her, I was able to restore her confidence and worth in me. But the enemy ultimately stepped in and brought another man into her life who was confident like her new found identity and she succumbed to the temptation, instead of honouring the commitment she made to you and waiting patiently for you to heal the way she had. Lillian gave in to her passions, instead of helping you heal and honouring the covenant you had both made as one flesh to me. For that, all I can say to you is I'm truly sorry that the enemy won that battle."

"She never gave me closure, to this day I don't know if she even loved me at all." I replied, "all I wanted to do was move on. But didn't find anyone I could move on with."

"Gideon," Jesus said, "All the people that came into your life were there to show you that you needed to heal, people are not band aids. Marriages aren't about two broken pieces coming together to make one. Marriages are supposed to be based on two people who are complete in me and come together as one flesh in the same way I love my church and unified myself to all of you by becoming one of you, all for the glory of the Holy City which is my home and yours." He paused for a minute, to make sure I took in every word He said. "Satan may have won the battle, but I've already won the war."

He raised His Hands to me. "I love Lillian and I love you too... this much." He pointed to the holes in His Hands where the nails had pierced Him. "I died for Lillian and I died for you too, you are each like lost sheep to me and I want to rescue all of you." He put his other hand on my shoulder now. "I promise you Gideon, if you just trust me, and give me your hand... I will work all things for good in your life, even this, and keep walking with you according to the purpose I have for your life."

"I'm not expecting perfection Gideon," Jesus said, "just do your best from the heart, and allow me to do the rest."

"Can we go back now?"

"Not yet..." Jesus replied. "There's something else that happened here, we need to conquer that together.

Chapter Seven

M**emory 4**

Ezekiel 36:26

I will give you a new heart and put a new spirit in you, I will remove from you your heart of stone and give you a heart of flesh.

"Prior to your divorce," Jesus said, "something else happened here that had an immense impact on you."

He took a deep breath, and when He exhaled, His breath filled the entire house in my memory with tiny golden sparks like flames. The scene reminded me of Pentecost when the disciples were blessed with the Holy Spirit in the form of tongues of fire. I knew what Jesus was talking about, I had been avoiding this memory my entire life from the second it had happened; it had been ten years, and still I wondered what life would've been like if I hadn't lost her. I imagined her with the same beautiful eyes that made me fall in love with Lillian, the same black hair, the same goofy smile; just as well because Lillian was far better looking than me. But, I imagined she would have my hands, my strange walk and my unique sense of humour. Life would've been so different if I hadn't lost my daughter, mainly because I wouldn't have lost myself...

"Yes," I replied. "This house contained both the best and worst parts of my life, kind of like the opening line to that Dickens novel..."

"Gideon..." Jesus smiled at me. "It's time to let that go." He waved his hand and the background of my memory shifted at high speed like the rewind button on a DVD player.

Jesus took me back to the morning I found out that Lillian could be pregnant, we were in bed and she got up with much urgency as she was feeling nauseous. I got up to see if she was ok.

"Do you think it's something you ate?" I asked her.

"No..." She washed her face, and looked at me while composing herself. "I think I'm pregnant."

"What?" My heart started pumping with excitement. "Are you serious?"

"I'm not sure," she said, "but all the early symptoms are there."

"I'm going to be a father?" I had always wanted to have a daughter, and I was already imagining how much more beautiful life was going to become with a little girl keeping me up at night.

"Gideon," Lillian replied. "Let's wait for confirmation please."

"Lillian, baby, this is the best news I have ever heard in my life," I kissed her.

It was too late though, my mind was made up and my heart was already set. I rushed out and bought her two pregnancy tests, everywhere I walked people were staring at me, because I'm pretty sure I had this perpetual silly grin on my face.

Gideon Daniels, who had done nothing of much importance was about to become a father, nothing else mattered in the world, all of a sudden, much less the judgemental looks of my fellow human beings who had no idea that the most important person in my life was going to be born in the next few months. She took home pregnancy tests and they had both come out negative, but yet her symptoms persisted. So I booked an appointment with our doctor and two weeks later, we went for a scan.

"Congratulations," Dr Garrison said with a smile, "you're six weeks pregnant."

"Thank you God!" I screamed and jumped up with utter delight.

Nothing else mattered from that moment on, my entire life revolved around my child. I wanted a daughter and had made all sorts of plans to prepare for her arrival. We had discussed names already, just like our child would have parts of us combined, so would their names reflect this. We agreed that if we had a boy, we would name him after our father's, John-Mark Daniels, and if we had a girl we would call her Gillian, a part of her and a part of me combined. Life had suddenly taken on a whole new meaning, our unborn child had suddenly become a band aid for our cracking relationship, which had suddenly taken a back seat. But just like a cracked glass will always be a cracked glass no matter how much you stop looking at the cracks, so was my relationship with Lillian.

"Can you imagine how amazing it's going to be when we start experiencing the important events in her life," I said to Lillian one morning in bed. "Her first day of school, her first boyfriend..."

"Gideon," she sighed. "You don't even know if we are having a girl. What if we have a boy?"

"That's ok..."

"Can you please just stop talking and wait for our baby to be born?" I could sense the irritation in her voice.

"I'm sorry..." I replied. "I thought you were as excited as I am about this child."

"I am happy," she said, "but we don't have to keep talking about it all the time. I have to deal with the changes my body is going through to you know?"

I was upset, not because she wasn't right, but more because it was during this exchange that I realized Lillian and I weren't ever going to be truly happy, and that saddened me tremendously. But we were going to have a baby, and to me, that's all that mattered. She worked as the PA to a lawyer in Greenpoint, so we both got ready for work without saying much more to each other after her outburst.

"See you later," I said. "Love you."

"See you later," she mumbled and got into her car before driving off.

I had become accustomed to her cold shoulder, it had become a large part of our daily routine, but I had something else to look forward to now, so it didn't really bother me as much anymore. Five weeks had gone by and my usual routine of drinking hot chocolate and checking emails while listening to the breakfast show on KFM radio was interrupted by a phone call on my mobile number. It was Lillian, she never called me unless it was urgent. So I panicked immediately.

"Hello... is everything ok?"

"I'm in pain Gideon," she said in between sobs. "Please come fetch me and take me to the hospital."

I didn't bother saying another word, I explained to my boss that Lilian wasn't feeling well, went home to pick her up and rushed to the hospital with her, groaning.

"But you're only three months pregnant, much too early for this kind of thing.," I shouted while driving through traffic with my emergency lights on.

"I know..." She shouted, holding onto her belly. "Just drive! Please don't talk!"

Dr Garrison was already waiting with a team of nurses at the entrance when I pulled up the pathway to the emergency unit and the team promptly helped her onto a stretcher and wheeled her into the ward.

"Dr Garrison," I grabbed his arm. "Please save them both."

"I will do the best I can," he nodded before rushing off behind the team of nurses who had gone on ahead of him.

I had no idea how long they were in there, but it felt like a decade, as I paced around the waiting room, biting my nails, my hands were shaking as I tried to page through some of the magazines they had there. But I couldn't focus, all I could think about was Lillian and our baby."

"Mr Daniels," the receptionist said. "Dr Garrison wants to see you in his consulting room, you may go through." She smiled kindly and showed me the way.

I broke into a cold sweat, and my legs went weak as I dragged myself through the corridor before getting to his door, the letters of his name stared me in the face and blurred out of focus as I gathered up the courage to knock.

"Please come in," he said, opening the door for me. "And take a seat."

I could tell by the sombre look on his face, that he didn't have good news for me. In the few seconds it took for me to get from the front door to the seat, I had come up with a thousand variations of the devastating news he was about to give me.

"Dr Garrison, please don't stall, just tell me what happened." I was gasping, choking with the pain of each word as I spoke, anticipating the absolute worse.

"I'm sorry Gideon," he replied, taking a deep breath. "Lillian had a miscarriage, in short, her uterus was too weak to hold the baby, in the first trimester of most pregnancies, this is very common unfortunately..." He reached out and grabbed my hand over his desk. "I'm sorry."

"Thank you," I said, after a long pause, as I tried to process how deep his words had pierced me. "Can I go see my wife now?"

"Of course," he smiled and led me to the ward.

"I'm so sorry Gideon," her face was drenched in tears.

"It's ok Lillian," I kissed her on the forehead and just lay down next to her. "Please don't apologise, it's not your fault."

We just lay there in complete silence, holding each other physically, but spiritually we were no longer there, the same parts we gave of ourselves to form Gillian, died with her that day, and there was no coming back from something that was lost forever. Gillian died along with what was left of our relationship.

I WAS CRYING ON JESUS'S shoulder, the shock, grief and pain just overcame me once more just like the day it had happened. I felt utterly broken, or perhaps I was never fully healed and only realized it now.

"Gideon," He held my face in his hands, and breathed into my nostrils. "Give me the ashes of your scorched heart. Allow me to replace that heart of stone with one of flesh."

His breath went into my spirit and it felt like a warm blanket had warmed me from within. Jesus waved his right hand and the sleeve of his tunic covered us both, a strong wind blew beyond the tunic and I could hear thunder, and before I could process what was happening around us, we were back at the stone table. Jesus was standing before me, his eyes were like two flames, and he had the Bible opened in his hands.

"Gideon my son," Jesus said, "as I read to you from the book of life."

He closed the Bible, and sat down in front of me. His eyes went back to how I had always seen them, and he looked at me with that effortless look of complete love and empathy, his gaze could break anything. Nothing could stand before those eyes.

"Gideon," he said, "I can only do this for you, if you allow me to. Do you want a new heart and a new spirit?"

"Yes Lord," I replied. "Please Lord..." I sobbed.

Chapter Eight

M^{emory 5}

Psalm 34:18

The Lord is close to the broken-hearted and saves those who are crushed in spirit

"Walk with me," Jesus said, getting up from the stone table where we were seated.

"Where are we going?" I asked, heeding his instruction.

"Gideon," Jesus replied, smiling, "learn to trust without questioning me. I am taking you up your road to Calvary."

His response sparked a hundred more questions in my mind, but I kept them to myself and just followed Him as He had asked, learning to practice how to trust, something I had refused to do a long time ago. We walked onto a gravel road, where there were olive tree plantations on either side, the road was winding and gradually went into a sharp incline, but my focus was on all the people in plantations. They were laughing, singing and tasting the olives as they picked them into wicker baskets. No one looked tired, no one was sweating, they all just picked those olives as if it was the best thing they could ever do; like they were born just for that purpose. So far, I hadn't seen one unhappy face, no matter what people did here, they did it with the utmost joy.

"Gideon," Jesus said, "how much do you miss your father?"

"So much," I said, after a long pause as I realized that if this was heaven, I could see him. "Are you going to take me to him?"

"Be still, know who I am and trust my plan Gideon," Jesus replied with a warm smile. "Were you and your father very close?"

"Lord, don't you know these things that you are asking?" I replied.

"I do, but like any father, I like to listen to my children speak from the heart," he smiled at me.

"Not at first," I said, noticing that the road was getting steeper. "But as I got older, and matured, I learned to appreciate the sacrifices because with hard work, he made the best out of his life, and with limited resources managed to provide for his family better than I ever would've had I been in his shoes. For that he earned my utmost respect and admiration. I've always regretted wasting so much time in my youth not getting to know him."

"Tell me more about your father," Jesus asked, "what is your fondest memory of him?"

I was surprised to see that Jesus wasn't going to take me on a trip back to my memories, this time He wanted me to take Him on a trip into my heart, I was struck by this humble and touching act of just providing a listening ear this time.

"MY DAD WAS NEVER MUCH of a talker, he was always more of an observer," I replied, remembering fondly the times when I would go to him and know always that he would have wise words for me. "But whenever he did open his mouth, it would always have an impact and always be memorable." The road was getting steeper, and although I didn't feel like I had a physical body, I could feel a weight on top of me, like this walk was going to take its toll on me. Was this what Jesus meant by saying He was going to take me up my own road to Calvary?

"He was always a reserved man," Jesus said, with a look of pride on His face, like He was happy to see that I had recognized the man He had created when my father was born. "I'm not going to talk now Gideon... It's your turn to talk, tell me more?"

"He was a real tough guy, showed no emotion," I laughed, "he was after all a block man, sawing animal carcasses for a living, but on the odd occasion, with a well-timed joke at the tip of his tongue. My fondest memory of my childhood was when we would go on road trips, there was this one shop my dad would always stop at to buy our favourite snack, biltong. It was a little café next to the fish market in Johannesburg, it was called Snacks and Savouries, an old friend of my fathers who worked with him in his early days as a block man retired and bought the shop with his retirement money. But my dad said he used to make the best biltong in the world. I believed him, he was after all a butcher."

"Your father was indeed a fine butcher," Jesus replied.

"Those are my fondest memories, my dad buying biltong and snacking on it during our whole trip, while he played his awful music from his younger days at full blast on the radio, while my mom would bicker and complain about how the radio was too loud and ask him to drive slower." I laughed again, as my mind went back to those days of my childhood. "He of course wouldn't listen to her." Just then I noticed how strained I was as the road before us got even steeper. "Lord, can we stop for a little while?"

"Yes of course," He said, looking as fresh as if He had just taken a leisurely walk through a park.

"Sorry," I said, "I thought being dead would make things easier."

"I've walked my Calvary already," Jesus said laughing, "now I want to walk you through yours."

"What happens afterwards?" I hesitated, not sure if I was ready for the answer.

"Patience my dear Gideon," He laughed. "Now what is your biggest regret?"

"My biggest regret?" I sighed deeply. "Hey aren't you supposed to take me into another one of my memories?" I attempted to deflect the question.

"Gideon," He replied in such a serene tone. "I want you to take me on a trip this time, into your heart. What is that common saying you all cleverly came up with on earth? A problem shared, is a problem halved?"

"My dad was the first person to warn me against getting married to Lillian," I said, "we argued about it of course. I guess I too inherited my dad's stubborn streak. Against his will, I got married to her." Suddenly the sum total of how much I missed my father hit me, and the weight of the words left unsaid pressed all the more heavily on me.

"You can imagine how stupid I felt when I woke up to an empty house and realized with a big crash landing that my father was right all along." The memory of when I returned home after my divorce came flooding back to my mind. "But he didn't have one word of judgement for me, like the loving father that he always was in his own way, he just took me into his arms and welcomed me home like that story of the prodigal son. The tough butcher man I grew up with was gone, in his place was an emotional father who was happy to see his son."

When Lillian and I got divorced, I needed a new start, and with my parents on the verge of retirement. I wasn't like my father, I didn't have a drop of entrepreneurial blood in my body, the long hours, the incessant complaints from customers. In that respect, I was definitely not my father's son. But he still dreamt of entrepreneurial success and invested his life-savings in a new business. I didn't want to leave him alone in that business, especially because he was diagnosed with Scleroderma-Arthritis, so I decided to do a little bit of what he had done for me his whole life. Sacrifice. But unfortunately things didn't go well, five years later, and we were stuck in a sinking ship, playing pinball with our creditors, using nothing but a rapidly dwindling cash flow. Our creditors finally pulled the plug, and we lost the business. This bankruptcy became a catalyst for my dad's decline soon afterwards. He stopped driving, he stopped talking passionately about what he used to love; politics and business. He fell into a deep depression, and this only worsened his auto-immune disease. His muscles atrophied, especially around his shoulders to a point where he couldn't move his arms. His skin tightened, he lost his appetite, and getting him out of bed was becoming more and more of a challenge. My father's life was shrinking and fading from his body, slowly but surely, and for me as his son, it was one of the most painful things to witness.

"Tell me about the last outing you had with him," Jesus said, putting his arm over my shoulder, and imploring me to continue walking with him. "Tell me more about that?"

I recalled the memory to Jesus as if I was reliving it:

"Come on," I said to my parents, "let's go for a drive."

One of my dad's favourite places in Cape Town was the vineyards on the hills of Durbanville. Every time I drove through the hills of Durbanville, he would see the beautiful vineyards spread across the plains on the hills, I could see that distant look in his eyes. I imagined how his soul would travel back to his younger days, when he was healthy, experiencing all those stories of him swimming and fishing and taking care of the land on his father's farm.

"This reminds me of home..." He used to say every time, taking a deep breath. That would break my heart every time.

We had lunch at the wine estate that day, my mom had a picnic basket prepared, I had bought my dad's favourite bottle of wine and we shared a wonderful lunch together in the cool summer breeze, the sun blessing us with its radiating light and the fragrant smell of rosemary planted on the outskirts of the picnic site. That was the last outing we had before he died, two weeks later, my dad was in the garden, I stepped away from him for a split second and that's when it happened. He took a bad fall, and all I heard was a scream, I ran back and saw him face down on the concrete steps that led up to the swimming pool. There was some blood, I picked him up, he was so light, it was like I had a child in my arms. I rushed him to the hospital, luckily nothing was broken but unfortunately soon after this incident he picked up a bladder infection that quickly spread to his kidneys and because his immune system was already compromised and he had a weak heart, he deteriorated very fast.

"Your dad's heart rate is dropping too rapidly, we need to check his pacemaker." The Doctor said, "so we going to wheel him in for a quick procedure and make sure it's not that."

The time he spent in theatre felt like an eternity. Unfortunately, the minute I saw the Dr walk out of the theatre with the scrubs still on and that defeated look in his eye, I knew what he was about to say before he spoke.

"I'm so sorry..." He put his hand on my mother's shoulder. "Mr Daniels didn't make it."

I grabbed on to my mother and felt her break in my arms. I had never felt more alone like in that moment, because one of the only two human beings on this earth who loved me unconditionally was gone and wouldn't be coming back.

"Gideon..." Jesus wiped my face with the sleeve of his tunic. "Your father is very proud of you for looking after your mother the way you have." He smiled. "Your father is fine... I promise you. To you he lost everything on earth, but that's not true. Here he has gained everything he worked for. I prepared a place for him all along. Let go of the guilt, so that I can replace that guilt with strength."

"Can I see him please?"

"You will, but first, follow me..."

Chapter Nine

John 16:33
"I have told you these things, so that in me you may have peace. In this world you will have trouble. But take heart! I have overcome the world."

Memory 6

"Are we supposed to reach the top?" I asked.

"Yes Gideon," Jesus smiled. "Think of this as Calvary, and this time, you're going to walk it with me."

We had barely begun the ascent and I was already wishing we were at the top of this insurmountable hill that was before us. Jesus was showing no signs of physical struggle, despite not having a physical body, I was feeling all the aches and pains of someone who was notoriously unfit doing a hike.

"Gideon," Jesus said, "I need to go on ahead because I am preparing something for you at the top."

"You're going to leave me alone here?"

"I never left my disciples when I left earth and ascended here," He put his hand on my shoulder. "I won't leave you either, I was with them and I am with you... until the end of age. As you continue, think of all the times you thought you were alone, especially the times when you were afflicted with pain and offer it up to me. I in turn will put it in your spirit and remind you of how I saved you from that."

Before I could say another word, I noticed him walk on ahead of me, his gait so effortless, and in the same instant he was gone. I had a heightened awareness of my surroundings; the sound of the gravel crunching beneath my feet, the feeling of the gentle breeze on my skin.

The distinct incense fragrance that ushered me into the Holy City was all of a sudden present in the air. I had always been a huge fan of that song by Simon and Garfunkel Sound of Silence, but at this moment for the first time in my life, I knew exactly what it meant. The sounds of silence were the cries of a man's soul, searching for meaning. Birds were flying overhead, and the sound of their wings flapping was so loud, I was tempted to go and hide myself, a lady bug landed on my hand. I was at least one thousand times bigger than this little insect, but when I realized, how despite it's size, that lady bug by fulfilling its purpose for the kingdom of God, was equally valuable to the Lord; I felt prodigiously smaller than it.

A sharp pain hit my forehead like an arrow and I fell to the ground, held my forehead in despair. My mind went back to the day I was sitting on my neighbour's wall at the age of seven. I was playing with a little yellow aeroplane that I had pulled out of one of those kinder joy chocolate eggs my mom had bought for me.

SWISH!!!

I imagined myself in the pilot seat flying high into the sky, to a world where the clouds were made of chocolate and rain honey. In my mind at that age, nothing was impossible, with that aeroplane I could go wherever I wanted and could be whoever I wanted.

The aeroplane slipped out of my hand, and as a reflex action I lunged backwards to try and catch it, within seconds I had fallen out of my childhood day dream and onto the cold, hard reality of my neighbour's driveway on the other side of the wall. I hit my head on a pot plant she had there and cracked my forehead open. The searing pain made me scream so loud it echoed in my ears. Blood flowed into my eyes, but I could see my dad rushing to my aid; he bundled me up in his arms and carried me home. My mother was ready with towels and Mercuro-Chrome, hoping it was just a scratch and they could nurse me back to health. But they soon realised the gash was much deeper than they had hoped and rushed me to hospital, two hours later I came back home after wetting the doctor's bed and getting seven stitches to patch up my cracked forehead.

"Gideon..." I heard Jesus's voice in my mind, "I know your suffering. Look..."

I saw Jesus imprisoned after the violent scouring. He had tears in his eyes, but his expression remained solemn and he remained silent while the Roman soldiers continued to insult and beat him.

"Hail king of the Jews!"

"Every king needs a crown!" One of the Roman soldiers emerged from the mob with a bunch of thorns he had twisted into a headpiece. "I crown you Jesus, king of the Jews!" He placed it on Jesus's head and hammered it into his skull with the butt of his whip. Jesus's screams were deafening, as I saw the thorns embed deeply into his skull, and trickles of blood poured from his head into his eyes.

"Gideon..." Jesus said, "I know your pain."

The visions stopped and the pain disappeared, I got up and continued climbing the hill. I couldn't forget the sight of Jesus's face contorting in pain as they crowned him with those thorns. Jesus had given me a glance into his own heart and showed me the depth of what he had done for each and every human being on earth. A dark cloud descended over the hill, and a brisk wind stirred in the air, for the first time since arriving in the Holy City, I felt unsettled and wondered if I was on an ironic climb to hell. A large snake slithered onto my path and its head was upright, it had black eyes and long fangs that protruded past its mouth. I was terrified because this snake was staring at me with menacing intent, and it hissed so loud that it made the earth shake beneath my feet.

"You don't belong here..." the snake's voice sounded demonic. "Don't make me come back and kill you again..." The snake was laughing and opening its mouth to expose all its fangs.

The trembling beneath my feet got worse, I lost my balance and fell once more, my back hit the hard gravel and it sent shockwaves through my body. I was translocated once more to Jesus's passion. This time I saw him carrying the heavy cross on his broken body. He was out of breath, his eyes were swollen shut, and his body was red from all the blood he had lost through the gashes all over his body.

"You!" A Roman soldier shouted to someone in the crowd "Help him!"

I NOTICED JESUS LOOKING up at the Roman soldier, and my point of view shifted to what he was looking at. From Jesus' perspective, that soldier's eyes were black just like the snake's eyes that had slithered onto my path, the soldier was sniggering and his voice was deep and hollow like a demon's, again like the snake's voice when he spoke to me. I was consciously back on the hill with the snake again, and a flash of thunder tore through the dark cloud above us. Another flash of lightening hit the ground between us and split the earth, the snake's hissing turned into a full blown, blood curdling scream. I saw an angel flying from behind the dark cloud and land between us.

"Get behind me satan!" Jesus's voice thundered through the sky. "Your time is running out, I have disarmed you and now I am going to defeat you once and for all. No more will you tempt and torment my people! Michael seize the serpent and toss him into the pit!"

So that angel was Archangel Michael, he was as tall as Gabriel, whom I had met earlier, but he was much bigger in stature, he was muscular and looked like the finest trained soldiers in a sophisticated army. The snake was trying to bite him, but he dodged every attack and with a few swift and effortless movements, he seized the snake by the head and threw it into the crack that had emerged from the lightening. I could hear the bloodcurdling screams getting more distant and what sounded like a fire had erupted from beneath the surface of the ground. The earth closed up and the dark cloud dissipated. Archangel Michael smiled at me, he was dressed in golden armour that had red, blue and yellow breastplates. He waved before flying off again into the sky.

"Lord," I said, "that was terrifying!"

"Satan always tries to get in the way of the plans I have for all my children," Jesus responded, his voice filled the sky once more. "But only if my children would remember to call on me and not be afraid, I would've come to their aid. I have already overcome everything satan can throw at you. Now keep going... you're not far now."

Everything had returned to normal, the gentle breeze, the bright blue sky and the acute awareness of my surroundings; like everything that was created by God had emerged from hiding and was praising the Lord just by fulfilling their purpose according to who or what God had created them to be. I was staggering up the hill, looked up to the top and saw a bright light emanating from its summit. A sharp pain ripped through my right leg. I fell once more to the ground rolling back a few meters.

"Lord!" I cried out. "What's happening?"

"There's one more thing I want you to come to terms with before I can allow you to come up here," Jesus replied. "Everything that happens to my children physically, has a spiritual implication. By that same token, for healing to be complete, the spirit must heal together with the physical wounds. Don't lose heart my son."

The pain was so intense that I passed out, and entered into a dream-like state. In my dream, I went back to the day of the accident, when I suffered a life-changing injury that distorted everything I believed myself to be. A few months after my divorce, I had seen Lillian with her new boyfriend and it left me particularly upset that she had just moved on without even giving me a second thought, like I had meant nothing to her.

It was a Saturday, I had finished work early, and the memories of the life we had shared were haunting me, instead of going home like I should've done, I went to the pub and drank until the memories had faded into my drunken oblivion. I needed to set myself free from the confinement of my own head. There was a cloud of cigarette smoke covering the bar area, I sat and just kept ordering drinks, with each one, hoping to drown another memory of Lillian and I. I had no idea how I was going to move on with my life.

"Buddy," the barman said, "I think you've had enough for today, maybe come back another time?"

"Ok..." I slurred, to my surprise.

"Can I arrange with a taxi service to get you home safely?"

"Thanks buddy..." I replied. "You're probably the only person in the world right now who cares about what happens to me. But I'll be fine. I live just up the road."

I stumbled out of the front door, my mind was numb but heavy with the weight of sadness and whisky. My legs were heavy like I was walking through mud, and everything around me sounded like it was so far away, like I was stuck in a bubble. I was too drunk and lost in my distorted reality to notice I had stepped off the pavement, and was stumbling on the road...

Beep! Screech! Crunch!

All I could remember was the searing pain of when the car hit me. I don't know how far up I was lifted, but hit the road with a serious thud, my scraped skin felt like it was on fire as I rolled a few meters forward. I had a throbbing pain all down the side of my body that left me motionless. I was dizzy, nauseous, and wondered if this was the end of it all.

"Someone call an ambulance!"

I recognized the barman's face, hovering above me. I was floating in and out of consciousness. I had no idea how long I was laying there for, it felt like an eternity, but finally the ambulance sirens cut through the quiet of the dark night and drowned out the curious chatter of the people passing by.

"Can you move?" The paramedic asked, touching various parts of my leg to access if I had a spine injury.

Not really... But I can feel everything," I groaned, the impact had sobered me up, and the pain was gradually increasing.

"From what I see here, you've either got a broken pelvis or a broken femur," the paramedic concluded. "We going to give you a shot of morphine, then roll you onto a stretcher and take you to the nearest hospital." The other paramedic brought the stretcher out. "Mr Daniels...I'm sorry but this is going to hurt."

No sooner had he finished speaking after giving me the morphine shot, than he had rolled me onto the stretcher. That was by far the worst pain I had ever felt in my life. My screaming echoed through the neighbourhood, and I passed out. I woke up in hospital, to learn that I had suffered a broken hip and a fractured femur. I remember lying in hospital feeling broken emotionally, spiritually, psychologically and now physically.

I literally felt like half the man I used to be, and I remember wondering in that moment, if I wouldn't be better off dead? Jesus translocated me once more to his crucifixion. Each time I saw a soldier drive a nail into each one of his extremities, I could feel the screws in my own leg throbbing with pain. The sound of Jesus' cries of pain, echoed in my ears and it all just made me realize that every human suffering can be offered up to him who suffered it all first. I could hear some of his last words, that rung across the sky...

"Father... forgive them for they know not what they do!"

"It is done!" He shouted moments later, and his head bowed down as he gave up his spirit.

"Lord make it stop!" I shouted, with tears in my eyes.

"Gideon," Jesus replied, "none of what you have gone through is the sum total of who you are, especially not to me. You are more than your failures, you are more than how this world has broken you, I have delivered you from all of this on the cross in Calvary, I gave up everything because nothing to me is more important than the salvation of my children."

"Gideon"... He was standing at the top of the hill, taller than the angels. His robes were bright white and the golden sash around his waist sparkled. He stretched out his hand to me and helped me to my feet. "You made it," he smiled.

"Only because I took your hand," I replied.

"You are finally beginning to understand the life I so desperately want to give all my children," he kissed me on the forehead and gave me a hug. I felt rejuvenated by his presence. There was no more pain, no more regret, no more tears, no more bitterness, I had heard my whole life about being reborn; in that moment, when Jesus kissed me on the forehead. I felt reborn in my spirit."

"Thank you Lord," Almost by impulse I fell to my knees.

"At ease my son," he took me by the hand and summoned me to my feet.

"Can I ask you something?"

"Of course..." He replied.

"Why did you forgive your killers?"

"Gideon," he laughed, "they didn't kill me, I willingly gave up my life. When you know the outcome of something, and know how all the pieces are going to fall into place. Then no matter what happens, we know its mere distractions. I put sin to death on the cross with me. No man is a slave to sin anymore, unless they choose to stay in sin. Not forgiving my killers as you put it and refusing them the same gift I died to offer to the world, would defeat the purpose for which I gave up my life. By forgiving them, I have dealt satan the final blow, because even though he used them to try and get rid of me, I conquered death and forgave them so that they too could have a chance to get away from satan, if they choose to. With me, everyone gets a second chance, even my enemies."

Chapter Ten

John 10:10-14
The thief comes only to steal and kill and destroy; I have come that they may have life, and have it to the full. I am the good shepherd. The good shepherd lays down his life for the sheep. The hired hand is not the shepherd, and does not own the sheep. So when he sees the wolf coming, he abandons the sheep and runs away. Then the wolf attacks the flock, and scatters it. The man runs away because he is a hired hand and cares nothing for the sheep. I am the good shepherd; I know my sheep and my sheep know me."

"What is this place called?"
"Salvation hill," Jesus replied.
"It's beautiful..."

The view from the top was breath taking. There was a valley just beneath the hill, unending patches of green stretched across it's plains, and trees of all sizes lined either side of the river that ran through it. The waters had a melodious tune like a hymn as they rushed through the river banks; even the waters praised The Lord with their flow. Beyond the edge of the horizon I could see earth, not in the same way I had seen it in Geography class; From where I was standing I could see so much more than just a blue ball with green patches on its surface spinning on its axis. I had always heard the term "war in the spiritual realms", but for the first time I could actually see that war. There were angels and demons literally fighting for the soul of each and every human being on earth; swords, shields and flaming arrows all around each person, as they carried on with their everyday lives.

There were those who chose to walk in darkness, they appeared like dark spots on earth's map. They were the ones who lived for themselves alone, killing, stealing and destroying everything and everyone on their rise to the top. There were demons surrounding each one of them, with what looked like hooks embedded in their spirits, and the demons were controlling their every move like puppet masters. Then there were those who roamed the earth like torches, there was a bright light shining from within them, these were the ones who lived their lives humbly and were always looking to make a difference, and help those around them. There were angels surrounding these souls, fighting to keep the demons away from them, and also helping them up and pushing them to keep going on times when they did fall. But the vast majority of human beings on earth belonged to the last category, they had light but it was very dim, and flickered from time to time, alongside each of these flickering souls, was a demon and an angel, pushing and pulling on them to try and win them for each of their respective sides.

"Each one of my children had the fire of the Holy Spirit placed within them when they were baptized as babies, but I also gave each one the act of freewill so they can choose to stoke that fire and keep it burning or ignore it until it fades and dies," Jesus said. "Choices are very important Gideon, because not only do they direct the steps of your earthly lives, but as you can see each choice either equips or disarms the enemy who is the father of lies and comes only to steal, kill and destroy my children."

I LOOKED AT THE FACES of each person. Those with the Holy Spirit fire burning brightly within them had these beautiful smiles and serene expressions, those whose fire had faded and were completely under the power of darkness had these hollow eyes and sullen facial expressions, and those who were in the spiritual tug of war, had anxious and confused expressions, like they were looking for something but not sure what that was.

"Lord what's going to happen to all these people?"

"Darkness only exists when light is absent," Jesus replied. He beckoned me to follow him. "If only my children would recognize me and take my hand, I would lead them out of all darkness and command my angels to accompany them as they continue to walk with me."

"Where are we going?"

"It's been quite a journey for you to get here," He smiled. "How are you feeling?"

"It's been a painful but liberating journey," I replied "Thank you, I feel a peace that I had never known before."

"Shalom Gideon," he put his hand on my shoulder. "Now that you have faced some of your fears and let go of some of your burdens, it's time for you to meet two people who are longing to see you."

I followed Jesus down the other side of the hill, and we followed a pathway that led right into the valley we could see from the top. When we got to the river, I noticed how clean the water was, and the melodic rush of the waters entered my soul and washed away whatever was left of the past I had just left on that hill. I dipped my hand in the water and felt it running through my fingers; it was neither ice cold, nor hot, but at a perfectly soothing temperature.

"Drink of that water Gideon," Jesus said, "and you shall never thirst again."

I took a handful to my mouth, it tasted sweet but pure, the moment I drank of that water, I could feel it quenching parts of me that I never knew were lacking life. I saw children playing beyond the palm trees on the other side of the river, it reminded me of my own childhood, when I frolicked for days on end, without a care in the world. How I missed those times.

"You can feel that way again Gideon," Jesus said, "we are almost there now."

He pointed at a beautiful house just up ahead. The house was made in gold and stood on a rock, separate from the other houses that surrounded it. The entrance opened to a lush garden with lavender and geraniums planted on either side of the front door, giving off their heavenly scent that filled the air and gently ushered us in. The distinct riffs of 60's era rock and roll guitar and the unmistakable sound of Elvis Presley's voice welcomed us to the front door, it took me back to my childhood years, and thanks to the music, I knew exactly who was going to be standing behind the front door of this beautiful house.

"Dad!"

"Gideon..." We didn't even pause to see if we looked different to each other, we just hugged. A long, beautiful hug restored all the lost years of connection that occurred between us since his death.

"How I have missed you," I replied, "mom and I still talk about you all the time."

"I know," he smiled. "Abba has shown me."

"What's it like from here? Do you miss us?"

"When we get here, if we don't forfeit our place," he replied. "We remain with our loved ones in spirit, through prayer. I could feel your heartbeat and your mom's right here every day because I was praying earnestly for you both. Occasionally, Abba will allow us to descend like angels to reach you, but for the sole purpose of restoring his peace to the hearts of those we have left behind. To reassure them that we are in his care now. This is home Gideon, this is where we belong. Not earth."

Jesus gave me a reassuring nod.

"I don't think mom has found peace yet," I replied.

"I will send someone her way very soon," Jesus replied, smiling. "So John, I can't help but notice the enticing smell of your food, what's on the menu?"

"Lamb stew, homemade bread and of course our delicious home grown wine," my dad said, his enthusiasm was palpable. "I hope you're hungry?"

"Starving," I replied, "after that climb."

"After Calvary, there's only reward my son," he touched my face just like he used to when I was a child.

"I see you're still an Elvis fan," I laughed.

"I only allow it because it helps him cook better," Jesus replied, laughing.

"Since when do you cook?"

I've always dreamed of becoming a chef," my dad replied, revealing a side of him that I had never known before, because I always knew him as the owner of the butchery, who planted lemon trees and built a chicken coup in our house garden as a hobby. "When I got here, Abba appointed me the head chef of the children's home; my dreams didn't die, they were just with Abba for safekeeping."

"Children's home?" I asked.

"Yes," Jesus replied, his gaze became distant and I noticed tears welling up in his eyes. "For all the unwanted and defenceless babies who are killed, and children who are brutally murdered by the spirit of death that roams the earth to sow destruction on my children to rob them of their faith in me. Each one belongs to me and I reserve a special place in this home for them." My dad comforted him.

"Thank you John." He nodded and grabbed my dad's hand on his shoulder. "Shall we eat?"

My dad walked us through his house, to the dining room, where he had set a table for us already. There was a menorah on it, with candles lit. I knew this was a Jewish custom, but had no idea what it all meant. The food looked amazing.

"Today is Pesah," Jesus said, "or as they say in English, Passover, a very important time for the Jewish people, when they commemorate their liberation from slavery in Egypt, in obedience to My Father's command that they would celebrate their liberation for all generations."

"I never understood the connection," I replied.

"Despite giving up my life as a new covenant for the whole world," Jesus replied, "I've never forgotten my Jewish roots, nor the nation of my people My Father chose for me to be born into, and it is his will that the entire world is reconciled to Him with the Jewish nation through me." Jesus went on to explain in depth how he was the word of God made flesh by the Holy Spirit after his father chose Israel as the nation for him to be born into. He clarified how through his life, God came down to redeem His creation to Himself by the power of the Holy Spirit.

"The enemy has sowed much division amongst my children, using confusion because they don't love each other the way I have loved each and every one of them," he said. "I have no favourites, every single human being was created in the image of my father, and when the enemy succeeded in tempting man to fall away from him, he had to come down himself to earth and conquer every weakness that the enemy uses against his children. That was my mission on earth, and now that I have conquered everything the enemy could use against man, including death, I am the way, the truth and the life, by which all of my father's children have become my children too, through me they can conquer too with my strength and not their own. That's why I told my disciples when I was on earth, if you have seen me, you have seen my father because through the same Spirit that hovered over the waters at the beginning of creation, we have become one substance; Father, Son and Holy Spirit, three persons, one spirit."

John 14:9

Jesus answered, "Don't you know me Phillip, even after I have been among you such a long time? Anyone has seen me, has seen The Father. How can you say, show us The Father?

"Consubstantial," I said, remembering this word from the church services I attended throughout my childhood.

"That's why they are called the trinity," my father replied.

Genesis 1:1

In the beginning God created the heavens and the earth. Now the earth was formless and empty, darkness was over the surface of the deep, and the Spirit of God was hovering over the waters.

We had a delicious and memorable meal, where Jesus taught me all about the Jewish Passover. The significance behind every part of the celebration and how he became the atoning Passover lamb for the world to be in-grafted with the Jewish nation for eternal salvation through him.

Romans 11:22-24

Consider therefore the kindness and the sternness of God: sternness to those who fell, but kindness to you, provided that you will continue in his kindness. Otherwise, you will also be cut off. And if they do not persist in unbelief, they will be grafted in, for God is able to graft them in again. After all, if you were cut out of an olive tree that is wild by nature, and contrary to nature were grafted into a cultivated olive tree, how much more readily will these, the natural branches, be grafted into their own olive tree!

"JOHN," JESUS SAID, as we stood side by side in the kitchen, each one washing their own dishes. "How about we go see the children now?"

"I thought you'd never ask," I'd never seen my father so excited before. "Follow me."

He led the way out of the house, and I followed, there were no words to describe the vastness of this beautiful city. So insurmountable, yet so personal, it was like each part of this place from the tiniest leaf to the limitless sky reached into our hearts and whispered a warm welcome that left an immediate memory which would last as long as the city itself. Eternal. We walked through a cherry orchard, and everyone greeted me as if I was an honoured guest, never before in my life had I ever been so welcomed anywhere.

"Feel free to pick some cherries Gideon," Jesus said, looking back over his shoulder.

"Thank you," they were the size of golf balls and were so sweet and juicy.

"We're here," my dad said, pointing at the entrance to the home.

True to the standard in the Holy City, the high walls were built in gold, and the big sign above the entrance gate read: YESHUA'S. Not only was that Jesus's name in Hebrew, but it also meant safety, which is where the children were now after a life of rejection, abuse and death. The sound of careless laughter and shrieks of excitement filled our ears as we got to the entrance.

"Go on," my dad said, opening the front door and allowing us to go in ahead of him.

I had no idea how many children were there, but the entire atmosphere was alive with their energy and joy. Children are the most honest people, they have no plans or ulterior motives, all they want is to live and enjoy every moment because they have complete trust and faith in their parents to take care of them, so that frees them of any burdens, and they can be exactly who they are, themselves.

"Children," my father shouted to get their attention. "I would like you to give our guest Gideon, who happens to be my son, a loud and joyous welcome."

"But, he's big like you," one of the little boys shouted putting up his hand. "Isn't he supposed to be little like us if you're his dad?"

"Unfortunately I got old, like my dad," I replied, we all couldn't contain our laughter at this young boy's innocent observation.

The children left their play areas and gathered in assembly before us, like a choir, and began to sing a welcome song. Their little faces and bright stares of infinite awe, made me think of my own little girl, Gillian. I wonder what she would've looked like if she had survived. Their voices sang perfectly in sync with another and their rhythm was on point, their song filled my heart with so much warmth and admiration.

"Beautiful," Jesus said, initiating a round of applause.

"Thank you little ones," my father dismissed them and his face lit up, like looking after those children summed up the entire purpose for his existence. "You can go back to playing until the dinner bell"

I mingled with some of the children, and stopped to admire some of their work; some were painting, others were drawing, others were learning to play the harp. The children were so friendly, many of them stopped to give me a hug.

"John are we ready for Gideon's surprise?"

"Yes indeed," my father replied.

"Natalie!" Jesus called. My sister emerged from behind one of the play areas.

"Where did you disappear to?" I gave her a hug.

"I was busy, and I'm pretty sure you were too," she smiled. "Come on, follow me."

She grabbed my hand, and I followed her outside, she had a picnic basked in her other hand. We stepped out into the garden, it was incredible. There were orange and granadilla trees lining the outer perimeter of the garden. Natalie pulled a blanket out of the basked and set it on the grass that between us.

"I can't remember the last time I went on a picnic."

"Glad we can make new memories bro," she playfully punched my arm.

"Why are there five places?" I asked, noticing that she was setting a fifth place on the blanket.

"There's someone I would like you to meet," Jesus said, arriving behind us with my father.

"Oh?" I replied, wondering who Jesus wanted me to meet.

He pointed across the garden and I saw a little girl on the swings having a lot of fun, swinging between the fruit trees. Her back was facing us, and her long black hair was waving behind her as she swung up and down.

"Sweetheart," my father called to her, "please come over here."

The little girl got off the swings and ran towards us. She was about four years old I guessed, and had the most angelic face I had ever seen that I was immediately drawn to. She had this beautiful smile that me wonder what her life had been all about before she got here.

"Hey little one," I said, crouching down to meet her eye to eye.

"Hello," she rushed into my arms and gave me a hug, a special hug that restored parts of me that I didn't know were missing.

"Wow," I said, running my fingers through her beautiful long hair. "Thank you so much for that special hug. What's your name?"

"She doesn't have one..." Jesus responded, and crouched beside me, touching her cheek. "Her parents didn't get a chance to give her a name."

"Oh that's awful," I replied.

"But her father arrived recently, so I'm hoping he will give her a name, so I can baptize her and make it official," Jesus said. "I love her and accept her either way, she is mine. But a name gives someone an identity, and creates a bond that lasts forever." I looked from Jesus to the child and back at Jesus again, before it dawned on me that this beautiful little girl was my daughter. It was Gillian!

"What?" I couldn't contain myself. I sobbed with complete delight and disbelief.

"Daddy," she said, "I've been waiting to see you for so long," blinking at me with her beautiful hazel-coloured eyes, filled with childhood awe.

"Honey I never found peace because I lost it when I lost you," I hugged and kissed her again and again, and took her into my arms once more. I was making up for all the time I lost because of never getting to meet her.

"You will have forever to enjoy my peace with her," Jesus said.

Natalie and my father joined us on the ground and we had a family hug. We sat down to eat, Jesus blessed the food and we had a blessed meal together, I could feel the Holy Spirit moving through the garden, filling us and binding us with chords of love that couldn't be broken.

"I believe now an official baptism is in order," Jesus said.

"Woohoo!" Natalie stood up and danced.

I could hear singing emanating from the sky, and when I looked up at the temple which provided all the light for the Holy City, I saw a choir of angels descending. Some were playing golden harps, others had flutes, and a group of them were singing beautiful hymns, praising the name of God, Adonai.

"Follow me," Jesus said, raising his hand, a wind picked up, causing a cloud to descend from the sky.

We stepped onto the cloud and Jesus carried us all high above the city. The view of the entire city from the cloud was incredible. The perfect balance of nature and urbanization, rustic and modern, reminded me of all of the greatest cities on earth, and yet at the same time, was majestically brand new to me. My sister and father were with me, I had my daughter in my arms and we were with Jesus, I can't remember my life ever being so perfect before.

The cloud descended and we climbed off and settled alongside a river bed. There was a gazebo set up with an altar, the angels then descended behind us and continued singing beautiful hymns about rebirth and finding new life in Our Saviour. Jesus being our High Priest, took his place behind the altar and began the service. Never before had I understood the significance of a church service. It's all about Jesus's life, death and resurrection. Much like a Jewish Passover, it was supposed to have so much more meaning that simply fulfilling a chore, or filling up our spiritual tanks. It was meant to be a celebration of our redemption, with our lamb of atonement alive and sovereign over us!

"Gideon," Jesus said walking into the water and beckoning for me to follow him into the water. "What is the name you want to give her?"

"Despite her mother and I separating," I said, "she is as much hers as she is mine, so for that reason, I will name her Gillian, in honour of the love Lillian and I once shared, which she is a fruit of."

"I will honour you for honouring her, my son," he smiled.

"Child," he said as I lowered her into the water. "I baptize you Gillian Daniels in the name of the Father and of the Son and of the Holy Spirit, and declare that I call you by your name and you are mine."

There was a round of applause, and the singing of the angels got louder. When we emerged from the waters, I got down on my knees and praised God for this miraculous experience that I had been graced with.

Chapter Eleven

Leviticus 20:6-7
"I will set my face against anyone who turns to mediums and spiritists to prostitute themselves by following them, and I will cut them off from their people. Consecrate yourselves and be holy, because I am the Lord your God."

I had no sense of time, and had no clue of how long I had been in the Holy City. But I was in no hurry to leave, spending all my time with Gillian, swinging on the swings with her, answering all her relentless questions about her mother, I obviously didn't want to tell Gillian about how she hurt me and ruin her mother's image, so I told her about the good things, like the way Gillian would always push me to do better and how she would always make me feel special on my birthday; I was relishing every moment being her dad, since I had lost the chance to be her father, and in a strange way, she was helping me see Lillian with new eyes, eyes that weren't ruined by betrayal.

"Daddy," Gillian said, giving me a picture she had drawn. "Why are you and mommy not friends anymore?"

I looked at the picture and there were three people on it, all named: "mommy, daddy and me." How do I explain to a child that her mother had left me for another man, without tarnishing the image of love she had for her? I couldn't do that, nor do I believe that's what the Lord wanted me to do.

"Sweetheart," I replied, "I was a little boy once just like you are a little girl. But as time went by, I grew up and became a big man. Sometimes big people don't stop growing and their hearts change over time too, and that's what happened to your mom, she outgrew me. Do you understand?"

"I think so," she said, scratching her chin. "Kind of like a caterpillar, it enters a cocoon and then it comes out with wings... it can't stay in the cocoon because the wings don't fit anymore." She jumped off my lap, spread her arms out and pretended she was flying away, before jumping right back into my arms.

"You're so much smarter than me already," I laughed and kissed her on the forehead.

"Gideon..." I looked over my shoulder and saw Jesus standing with my father and Natalie beside him.

"I love that you are having a good time with Gillian," Jesus said, "but your journey has not ended and must continue. Come with me."

"Sweetheart," I picked Gillian up, gave her big hug and a kiss. "I need to go with Abba now. Not sure if I will see you again, just know that no matter what, I love you more than you will ever know"

"I love you too daddy," she replied. "Don't worry about me, I'm here with Grandpa, Auntie Natalie and Abba."

"I know sweetheart," I replied. "I wish I had known all along."

Natalie stepped forward and took Gillian into her arms. I followed Jesus as he had asked, waving at my family, wondering if I would ever see them again and where I was going to go now. What did Jesus mean by my journey having to continue? Where was it going to end? Was he giving me a consolation prize before sending me to hell?"

"So," Jesus put his arm over my shoulder. "How do you feel, knowing now that you didn't lose your little girl?"

"Thank you Lord," I replied, unable to contain the tears of immense joy that were bubbling up in my spirit. "I've been restored beyond all expectations."

"Good," Jesus smiled. "Nothing that is offered to me is ever lost."

"Where are we going Lord?"

"There's one more memory that I need you to confront with me."

"What happens then?"

"Gideon, my son," he looked through me with his intensely loving gaze. "Have I not given you enough proof that you can trust me?"

"I'm sorry Lord," I fell to my knees. When I looked up, I saw a dove descend on him, and his entire presence glowed like the light coming from the temple at the top of the hill that provided the entire city with light and I could see flames at the edges of the dove's wings, like the way the tongues of fire are described in the Bible on Pentecost. The dove ascended from Jesus's shoulder, and descended gently on me.

"Everything is about to change for you Gideon," Jesus said, "Are you going to take my hand so I can walk you through it?"

"Yes Lord," I couldn't raise my eyes to him, but I raised both hands, and could feel his hands in mine picking me up from the ground.

"I'm going to give you a map that is going to lead you to a place outside of the Holy City," Jesus said, "be strong, take courage and follow my map faithfully, no matter what." He pulled what looked like a scroll from inside his right sleeve.

The scroll was sealed and when Jesus broke the seal, a bright light emanated from it as he handed it to me. I inspected the map carefully. There were pictures of places I had become familiar with, like the park where I had first met Gillian, the winepress where I had met some of the apostles, the stone table where I had gone on the trip through my past with Jesus. There was a blue line that Jesus wanted me to follow, that lead right out of the Holy City's entrance and stopped right outside the gate.

"Gideon," Jesus said and held both my hands in his. "Trust me, no matter what."

With these words, he stepped away from me and in instants he was gone from my sight. The place outside of the Holy City was labelled *Valley of Death*. When I came to the full realization that this is where the map was leading, I was certain Jesus was sending me to hell. But he did ask me to trust him, so with a heavy heart, acknowledging that I had decided to throw away the gift of life Jesus had given me by committing suicide, in that moment I resigned myself to that fate. Walking back through all the places I had encountered, retracing my steps since my arrival filled me with immense sadness because for some reason I was convinced that I wouldn't be coming back here. When I got to the entrance, I saw Archangel Michael standing like a soldier.

"Archangel Michael," I said, "why is Abba sending me to the valley of death?"

"Abba doesn't send anyone to the valley of death," he replied, "he has prepared a place for everyone here, but some people forfeit their place here by some of the choices they make."

"But I am sorry for doing what I did," I was in complete distress. "Why didn't Jesus forgive me?"

"Gideon," Archangel Michael said, opening a Bible and giving it to me. "Read psalm 91 and remember what Abba taught you about dressing his armour?"

"Of course," I did exactly what he had asked, and spoke those scriptures over myself, declaring them with all my heart.

"Walk by faith, not by sight, and you will not be removed from the path Abba has set for you." He opened the gate and smiled, almost as if he knew exactly what was going to happen.

Archangel Michael gave me one last reassuring look before beckoning me to be on my way. I stepped outside of the gate, and a cold breeze blew that sent shivers through my body. I looked over my shoulder, saw the Holy City entrance gates behind me and realized for the first time how important God's anointing was... because outside of the Holy City, I couldn't feel it as intensely anymore. I literally felt like I had stepped out of the protection of the Lord's Almighty shadow. I opened the map again, and continued on the journey, one reluctant step at a time. The path winded out and I turned a corner before going down a steep descent, despite my insides feeling like they were in knots with how unsettled I was feeling, I continued as per the directions on the map. The sky was getting darker and the breeze was picking up and turning into a brisk wind, just then I noticed a cottage at the bottom of the descent, there was a bright light shining through the window and since it was getting darker, I thought it would be a good idea to make a pit stop and continue at the first sign of light.

"Hello?" I knocked on the door.

"Hello?" A woman answered the door. She had dark hair and dark eyes, her face looked so familiar but I just couldn't remember where I had seen her.

"Sorry for stopping by unannounced," I replied, "I just came from visiting the Holy City and was wondering if I could stay here for a while until daybreak?"

"Ah Gideon," she said smiling. "Come in."

"Wow you know my name," I said, "Are you from the Holy City too?"

"Well yes," she said. "But I decided to stay here."

"Do I know you?" I asked. "You look so familiar?"

"Maybe we crossed paths while we were both on earth?"

"So what do you do here?" I asked. "Why do you prefer it here?"

"Let me quickly get us some tea," she said, and disappeared into what I assumed was her kitchen and returned almost as fast as she disappeared. "I advise people, like a spiritual guide," she handed me a cup of tea.

"Oh that's fascinating," I replied, tasting the tea, it had this incredible mint aroma and was sweet like honey, but burned inside of me like a fire.

"It's fascinating indeed," she replied. "Everyone wants guidance, but not everyone finds it, that's where I come in... I make sure everyone knows exactly where they are going."

"Sounds like an important job," I replied, finishing the tea.

"Do you know where you're going Gideon?" she asked.

"No," I replied, "but I am trusting Jesus to lead the way."

"Of coursssssseeee," she said, her eyes peered straight into me, but I couldn't shake how familiar her face was. "Wouldn't you like to get an idea of where you're going, you know, I've helped others... If you would like, I can help you too?"

"That would be amazing," I replied.

"Great," she said, smiling. "I'm going to get my things, then I will call you to come through to my consulting room."

I looked around at her cottage, it was small but cosy, the strange thing was that there was nothing anywhere about Jesus or any indication of the Holy City anywhere. There was a bookshelf across from where we were seated, and there were books about every topic imaginable from astrology and chakra healing, to tarot cards and energy alignment. There were dream- catchers hanging from the ceiling, and other strange ornaments that I had seen before but had no idea what they were used for. I got a sudden uneasy feeling and the hairs on the back of my neck stood up.

"Come through," she said.

Her voice was so soft and gentle, she had this alluring smile and if I was honest, Jesus truly hadn't answered my question whenever I asked him where I was going from here, my curiosity got the better of me, and if this woman was able to tell me where I was headed, if it wasn't to a good place maybe I could still do something to change that. So I got up and walked to the room where the light broke through the darkness and illuminated the path of the dark corridor.

"Just lay down and relax," she said, "don't open your eyes, because not everyone is prepared to see the things of the spirit world, and the objective is for you not to be overcome with fear."

"Just focus on the sound of the water, washing away all your cares and bringing in with it inner peace," there was this soft background music that accompanied the sound of waves crashing.

A wave of relaxation was coming over me, when I felt a sudden warmth entering my nose, I panicked and opened my eyes to find the woman hovering over me with her mouth wide open over mine as if she was about to take possession of my soul; her eyes were hollow, and her teeth were like fangs.

"No!" I leapt off the massage bed and tried to run out of the room, but the door was locked.

"Too late Gideon!" Her voice sounded like a demon, and she laughed so loud it echoed,

"Jesus gave you a life and you threw it away, you're one of us now! Welcome home!"

The floor beneath my feet cracked open and I fell through, into this long descending vortex. There was a raging fire around me, the flames crackled in my ears, there were desperate and relentless cries that echoed from above and beneath me.

"Welcome Gideon!" A voice deeper and more sinister than anything I had ever heard before reverberated from the depths and shook me to the core.

"No!" I shouted. "Jesus, help me! Please!" It felt like I was falling faster than before, and I could feel the heat of the flames getting closer and closer.

"Repent my son," Jesus's voice cut through the terror, and went straight into my heart. "Repent of all your involvement in the occult with all your heart, and trust me."

"Lord, I am so sorry," I said, "do your forgive me?"

"Seventy times seven," Jesus responded, "as long as you repent with all your heart. Michael, go get him."

Jesus's voice faded and moments later, I could feel myself being hoisted upwards out of the vortex, I was so afraid that I closed my eyes and only when the crackling of the flames and the screams dissipated completely did I open my eyes again, and noticed that I was in the arms of Archangel Michael, flying high above the valley of death and past the gates of the Holy City before descending.

"Thank you Archangel Michael," I said.

"All in a day's work Gideon," he smiled and gently put me on the floor.

Moments later, I noticed Jesus appearing before me, and I could think of doing nothing else except running over and falling into his arms like a terrified child into the arms of his father.

"Welcome home my son," he whispered. I was still reeling at what I had experienced, we just stood there in silence, looking each other in the eyes and despite having so many questions. I didn't know where to begin.

"Thank you for saving me Lord," I said, I bowed my head in reverence.

2 Corinthians 11:14
And no wonder, for satan himself masquerades as an angel of light.

"Gideon," Jesus said, "I don't send anyone to hell, some unfortunately follow the path that leads to hell, thinking it will lead them to where their souls are yearning to go, don't you remember where you know that lady from?"

"Remember soon after your divorce, you went with some friends to a festival, and ended up visiting a psychic?"

It all came back to me. I remember the day well; we had gone to a music festival, where they had beer tents and food stalls. I was feeling so lost, and just didn't know what to do with my life. I had lost my wife and my daughter, so when I saw that red tent, it was the dim light in the dark tunnel that was my life. So I walked in with a completely open mind, and allowed this woman to read my palms, and I also paid for her to take out a deck of tarot cards.

I didn't leave feeling much better because she had given all these obscure bits of advice that I could've just as well read off my horoscope for the day, but I was quite spooked by how accurate her reading of my life was.

"I needed direction Lord," I said, "I didn't know where else to go." I shrugged.

"Gideon," Jesus put his hand on my shoulder. "I was waiting for you to come to me, in church so I could give you that direction."

"I'm sorry Lord," I bowed my head once more, but this time in utter shame.

"The enemy masquerades as light in practices like tarot cards, astrology and the like, to lead both the one who practices them as well as those that consult them. The problem with walking into this kind of false light, is that it disguises the path to ruin with beautiful experiences that appeal to the senses but remove my Holy Spirit from the heart, which is my dwelling place in all my children. Why would my children trust more in the stars than me who created the stars? This false light enslaves my children using nothing but spiritual blindness and misguided choices resulting from counterfeit enlightenment, these two instruments are so much stronger than any chains the world has created." Jesus took a deep breath, "I am the way, the truth, and the life Gideon. I am the word made flesh, and I came down to earth as one of my children to save them from the false light that masquerades as my own, to lead them to destruction. Hold steadfast onto my word, and it will be as if you are holding onto my hand to keep you from being deceived by evil masquerading as good."

"Yes Lord," I replied, "If it's not too late... I will do that."

"Your journey is coming to an end here Gideon," Jesus said, "but there is one more person here who is so eager to meet you. Follow me."

Chapter Twelve

Luke 1:48
"For he has been mindful of the humble state of his servant; from now on all generations will call me blessed."

W e were en route to the temple right at the top of the hill, the centre of light for the Holy City. I knew better than to ask questions by now, so I just walked in silence with Jesus, happy just to make the best of each moment. One thing I learned since arriving here was that there is immense freedom in the unknown, if we can learn to let go of the past, embrace the present and leave the future in the hands of the one who created it.

"I'm so proud of you Gideon," Jesus said putting his arm over my shoulders, in the comfortable gesture I had become accustomed to.

"Thank you," I replied, "but why? I have done nothing to deserve your honour."

"It's not in what you've done, but what you are still going to do that I am proud of," he said. "You've finally embraced the gift of faith I've been wanting to put in your heart since birth, if you hold onto that gift and use it, you will finally complete the tasks I have for you to do and fulfil the purpose for which you have been created." (Ephesians 2:10.)

We arrived at the door of the temple, there was an angel on either side of it, dressed in full armour and holding a sword in each of their hands. The hilt was golden, emblazoned with the words: *ruach ha-qodesh* engraved on them.

"What does that mean?" I asked, pointing to the words engraved on the swords.

"It's Hebrew for Holy Spirit," Jesus responded.

"This is the temple of God the father, right," I said, "am I going to meet him?"

"No one comes face to face with my father, unless He so wills it."

The angels gave me a courteous nod, and stepped aside so that I could walk in with Jesus. It was the most beautiful place of worship I had ever seen. There was harp music softly filling the air, everything was in gold with the finest wood finishes. There were men and women all busy; some were cleaning, others were carrying chairs, and others were putting up golden sashes. No one was stressed, everyone was working with smiles on their faces in complete joy. All dressed in white robes.

"Why is everyone so busy?"

"All the angels and saints are preparing for the feast," Jesus said, "It's someone's birthday, and here we all celebrate birthdays with a banquet here, because we remember with great joy the day another one of heaven's children were created."

"That's beautiful," I replied.

"Follow me," Jesus said, and led the way through the entrance hall to a door that opened into a corridor.

Each person stopped what they were doing, and acknowledged my presence with a friendly smile and courteous greeting. I've never been so acknowledged anywhere in my life, if people on earth could acknowledge each other as they do in heaven, there would be peace on earth as there is in heaven. The corridor went much further than what met the eye, I couldn't see the end of it, but it was lined with doors on either side, and there were children rushing through the corridor, laughing and greeting Jesus by raising their hands to him. Each door was varnished to perfection, and had the exact same beautiful handles in gold; every door had a gold plate above it with a name engraved on it, and I was in complete awe. When I focused my attention back on where Jesus was leading, I saw him standing before an open door, waiting to usher me in. I looked over my shoulder, and noticed we were so far into the corridor that I could no longer see where we had come from, there was a bright light that emanated from the corridor and illuminated the entire corridor.

"Come in," Jesus said, ushering me through the door.

There was such a warmth that enveloped me as I stepped into the room, like the gentle rays of the sun on the first days of spring or summer after a cold winter. To my utter surprise, this was more than just a room, it was an entire house, complete with all of the best furnishings and comforts, simple but yet far better than anything I had ever seen on earth. Jesus walked in behind me, but went ahead of me to a door which led to a balcony.

"Mother..." Jesus said.

A woman walked in from the balcony, she was the most beautiful woman I had ever seen, and not beauty in the carnal sense. She had this complete grace about her that elevated her beauty beyond anything the world could ever quantify. She had dark hair and piercing brown eyes that looked through me in the most gentle of manners, her eyes reminded me of Jesus's eyes. Her gentle smile encompassed all the kindness that my imagination could contain, she was wearing a luminous white dress that was adorned with jewels of colours that I couldn't describe.

"Oh Gideon, how I have prayed for you," she stepped forward, gave me a hug and kissed me on the forehead, "the nights I spent praying with your mother for you to know my son as your saviour."

When her arms were wrapped around me, it took me right back to my childhood; I was about five years old, there was a thunderstorm and I distinctly remember seeing a flash of lightning descend from the overcast sky and it hit the open field alongside our house with a loud crack, it filled me with so much terror that it left me trembling. I started crying, and the only person I could think about was the woman who had nurtured me and protected me from birth, my mother. I ran into her arms and just stayed there until my trembling had subsided and my fears had dissipated. Being in Mother Mary's arms felt like being five years old again... in my own mother's arms.

"I don't know what else to say but thank you Mother Mary," I said.

"Let's have some tea," Jesus said.

"Yes please," Mother Mary replied, beckoning me to follow her out onto the balcony.

THERE WAS A TABLE SET on the balcony with tea and cookies, Jesus served us and I was admiring the breath taking view of the Holy City while savouring the refreshing lemon tea with the most delectable chocolate cookies I had ever tasted. There were beautiful flowers that lined every corner of the balcony, they gave off a scent similar to the one I had encountered when I had first arrived, which led me straight to Jesus.

"I've been looking forward to meeting you," Mother Mary said.

"I'm humbled Mother Mary," I replied, "thank you, but may I ask why?"

"Of course, she smiled, "your mother spiritually put you in my arms as a baby because she didn't know if you were going to survive and wanted to make sure your soul was in good hands. Jesus, please show him."

I could feel Jesus's hands on my head, and suddenly I could see my mother, she was much younger, younger than I could ever remember. She was on her knees at her bedside, crying and holding onto her rosary beads while deeply in prayer. I could hear her say: "Mother Mary, you watched your son die on the cross, as I am watching my son die now. Only you truly understand my heart, the deep wound that is in it. So I am giving my son to you, and I'm asking you to please speak to your son Jesus and ask him to heal my son, but let his will be done. I put my son into your arms and ask that you present him to Jesus so that his soul may be purified for heaven, even if he calls him home to be with him." Watching my mother cry for me was ripping me apart, my anguish became her anguish in that moment.

"Thank you," I said, Mother Mary wiped my tears.

"And now history has repeated itself," she replied with a deep sigh. "Jesus, please show him where his mother is right now..."

Jesus waved his hand and I saw a vision materialize before us like a hologram, I could see my mother, she was on her knees crying next to the hospital bed where I was lying unconscious, her face was wet with tears and her eyes were closed; she was praying intensely, clutching at her rosary beads. She was alone, and as I had always known her, didn't care at all for what everyone around her might think of her. I'd never met a more faithful person in my life, my heart ached as I remembered the times I ridiculed her for being so fervent in her faith, and always talking to others about church and her relationship with God.

"Do you see how her heart is breaking again, Gideon?" Mother Mary said, "When people choose to end the gift of life Jesus died to give them, their pain doesn't end, they just leave it behind for their loved ones to carry."

"I know you were in pain, I understand it and I was praying for you with your mother... I'm still praying for you." She caressed my cheek, in a way that reminded me of the secure love my own mother made me feel.

"Thank you Mother Mary," I grabbed her hand and kissed it.

"People reject me because they don't understand me," she said, her gentle voice was charged with emotion. When I saw those men mercilessly scourge and crucify my son, all I could remember was the words of Simeon when I presented Jesus in the temple; that his eyes had seen the Lord's salvation, and that he was destined for the falling and rising of many in Israel, and to be a sign that be spoken against, so that the thoughts of many hearts would be revealed," her eyes became distant, as if she was reliving that horrible moment in her life. "Truly Gideon, I tell you, Simeon's words came true. When that soldier pierced Jesus's heart with the spear, so was my heart and soul pierced." She was crying and showed me her heart, how it bled. "I am the mother of Jesus, and like any mother who loves and supports her child. I too love and support Jesus in his mission of salvation. I never asked God to make me Jesus's mother, but he chose me and in obedience to Him, I accepted His will and carried Jesus into the world for salvation, by the same way, those of the world who choose me, I will carry to my son Jesus so they can find the salvation that he obtained for all."

Luke 2:29-35

"Sovereign Lord, as you have promised, you may now dismiss your servant in peace. For my eyes have seen your salvation, which you have prepared in the sight of all nations, a light for revelation to the Gentiles, and the glory of your people Israel." The child's father and mother marvelled at what was said about him. Then Simeon blessed them and said to Mary, his mother. "This child is destined to cause the failing and rising of many in Israel, and to be a sign that will be spoken against, so that the thoughts of many hearts will be revealed. And a sword will pierce your own soul too.

"Gideon," Jesus said, showing me his heart too. "My mother's heart bled with mine when I was crucified, now mine bleeds with hers as I watch my people crucifying her with their words. Salvation has been obtained, and I am the way, the only way to eternal life. My Mother is only helping people to find me. Let the people take heed of the message she gave to the servants at the wedding feast of Cana, "do whatever he tells you."

We finished our tea, and Mother Mary gave me rosary beads, and together they taught me the rosary, and how powerful it is to meditate on the birth, life and death of Jesus Christ through the eyes and heart of his Mother Mary through praying the rosary. It was beautiful and powerful, the beads were gold and the rosary fit around my neck, I wore it like a necklace, to remind myself of Jesus and his blessed Mother, who carried Him to us, and now yearns to carry us back to Him.

Chapter Thirteen

Matthew 28:18 -20
Then Jesus came to them and said, "all authority in heaven and on earth
has been given to me. Therefore go and make disciples of all nations,
baptizing them in the name of the father, and of the son, and of the Holy
Spirit, and teaching them to obey everything I have commanded you.
And surely I am with you always, to the very end of age.

"Are you ready?" Jesus asked me.

"I'm not sure what you mean, but as long as you're with me," I replied.

Jesus put his hands on my shoulders, and I felt the fire of the Holy Spirit descend upon us like a dove and envelop us with his fiery wings, we were taken up in a gentle breath of wind, and trans-located to a room that I had not seen before. It looked like a dining hall, there was a long table set with bread and wine at its centre and there was an innumerable amount of people seated as if they were waiting for a meal to be served. I only recognized my dad, sister, Gillian, the apostles Peter and John as well as Mary Magdalene, who were all waving at me with the same enthusiasm as the first time they had seen me. I don't know if Jesus was going to send me to hell or not, but the one thing I would miss most about heaven, is the enthusiastic joy of just being alive in heaven that everyone had. Two feelings that were short-lived and somewhat foreign to me throughout my earthly life; joy and enthusiasm.

"Hello Gideon," an angel appeared behind me, greeting me courteously. "May I show you to your seat?"

"Hi there," I replied. "Yes please.

To my complete disappointment, I was not seated at the table with everyone else, the angel sat me on a table separate from the main table, and joined me on that same table, just the two of us. I couldn't hide my disappointment; 'is this the table of the condemned? Like one last meal before execution?' were some of the million thoughts that were racing through my mind.

"Do not be afraid Gideon," the angel said, no doubt reading the expression on my face. "Just trust the Lord."

Jesus took his place at the centre of the table that resembled the one on the famous painting by Leonardo Da Vinci about the Last Supper, only much bigger and with many more people. Everyone was chatting and laughing, but the minute Jesus took his place and remained standing, all the chattering came to a halt and we all focused our complete attention on Jesus who looked like he had a message for us. He greeted everyone courteously, and smiled.

"Family," he began, "for those of you who haven't met him yet, this is Gideon Daniels." He pointed me out and everyone turned to wave and greet with heaven's signature enthusiasm and courtesy. "Our enemy tried to snatch him away from my hands, but thanks to the many prayers prayed in faith over him, as well as what I found every time I looked past his pain to what was deep in his heart, satan's plans did not succeed. I saved him, just like I saved all of you, and wish to save every single person on the face of the earth."

Everyone cheered and a loud applause resounded throughout the room. "My plans for you were bigger than the enemy's traps, my plans for Gideon are bigger than any weapon the enemy has wielded against him!"

"Shalom, shalom!" Everyone shouted, clapped and cheered once more.

"Gideon," Jesus turned to look at me, "I have a plan for your life, "but it's up to you to accept that plan. I am going to give you a second chance to fulfil the plan I had for your life from birth. I love you Gideon, and I have called you unto myself; just like I commissioned my disciples before ascending here after my resurrection, to preach the good news of the gospel in word and in action. Making disciples of all those who accept the call of salvation from all nations. I've taken away your hurts, I've showed you that what was taken away from you was not lost. I left the Holy Spirit to be a helper to my disciples then, and that same Holy Spirit is still available to you, if you choose to accept the gift of my salvation. My dear Gideon, do you accept the call to preach the good news of the gospel, and by accepting my salvation be a witness to that same salvation for others who cross your path on your earthly pilgrimage, to find it as well?"

I saw him look at me with that immensely powerful, loving and penetrating gaze. Something within me just convicted me with such gentle force that I stood up and with every fibre of my existence and declared, "Abba, I accept."

There was more loud cheering, applause and a choir of angels entered the room with harps and filled the room with their beautiful music, praising and worshipping God. People were coming up to me, introducing themselves, congratulating me, and for the first time in a really long time, I actually felt like I belonged somewhere, and that was the best feeling in the world. I met the rest of the apostles, most of them were a lot taller than I imagined them to be when I heard their stories as a child. I was particularly fond of Saint Paul, he had a great sense of humour, and I remember him fondly as he was the patron Saint of the primary school I had attended.

"Thank you Gideon," Jesus said, interrupting our social gathering. Everyone returned to their places again and there was absolute silence once more. Jesus looked at me, gave a courteous nod and had a serious expression on his face. "Please be aware that the walk on this path that leads to the narrow gate which opens to heaven is not an easy one. The world is going to hate you as it did me, but you will have your brothers and sisters in me praying for you all the way; and as I promised my apostles, I will be with you to the very end. Do not be afraid. In times of great need, I will send angels to minister to you as they ministered to me when I was being tempted in the desert."

"Thank you Abba," I replied, falling to my knees and praising his name.

Jesus proceeded to break the bread and share the wine on the table with everyone, until everyone had their fill. People were talking to each other and it looked like a real family reunion, except there were no stereotypes, everyone was included and everyone was important. This looked like the kind of family reunion meal all people dream about on earth. Once the meal was over, everyone said good bye to me on their way out, as people made their way back to their respective places. Soon afterwards, it was just my father, my sister, Gillian, Jesus and I in the room, and we were all facing each other. Goodbyes are hard, even in heaven. I didn't want to leave and my heart was breaking to know that I was leaving heaven to go back to earth with all its inevitable insecurities and pit falls.

But I thought of my dear mother, who must be exhausted, and this brought me a little comfort. At least I knew my daughter would be here waiting for me when I return. I had a purpose again, and this time, no one would steal this from me, and that brought me great relief and joy.

"Well," I said, "I guess this is it huh? I hate goodbyes..."

"So do I little brother," Natalie had tears in her eyes, but smiled. "I will be praying for you always." She kissed me on the cheek and gave me a hug that made up for all the years we never got to spend together.

"Son," my dad said, hugging me next. "I will be watching you from afar. Always."

"And you my little angel," I said, scooping Gillian up into my arms. "I am going to take you with me in my heart." I held her so tight, and didn't want to let her go.

"I love you daddy," she said. "Please tell mommy I love her too, you don't know this, but she thinks about me sometimes."

"I will my angel," I kissed her gently, and when I put her down I started to cry, because it felt like I was losing her all over again.

They waved goodbye and walked off, taking pieces of my heart with them. Jesus put his arm around me and walked with me all the way to the entrance gate of the Holy City. He spoke to me about how much he loves each and every person on earth, and how much joy he experiences when one of us on earth turns away from darkness and back to his light. We spoke about his second coming, but he never told me the day or the hour, because that wasn't for anyone of us to know. But he did say that he wants us all to be prepared for his arrival.

"Thank you Gideon," Jesus said.

"No," I replied. "Thank you Lord." I hugged him with all my strength.

"Gideon," Jesus said, "remember to trust me. Keep your heart focused on me at all times, and you will recognize my light, even in the darkest of times."

"Yes Abba," I replied. "I will do my best."

I began my descent down the same stairs that I had taken when I first arrived, the steps that led to this monumental transformation in my life. I turned back and waved at him, before continuing, moments later, all I could see was clouds as I continued to descend, my earthly senses were slowly returning. I suddenly felt naked and utterly vulnerable, I was disappointed to be returning back to my human state, away from the glory of heaven. I could feel the push and pull between my flesh and my spirit starting to rage again. I then collapsed into that familiar vortex of air, and as I descended into that pocket of air, I could feel my lungs within my chest filling with air again as I descended into my motionless body lying in the hospital bed beneath me...

Proverbs 3:5-8

Trust in the Lord with all your heart, and do not lean on your own understanding. In all your ways acknowledge him, and he will make your paths straight.

TO LIGHT

"Everything is cracked, that's how the light gets in." – Anthem. Song by Leonard Cohen.

Chapter Fourteen

2 Corinthians 5:17
Therefore if anyone is in Christ, the new creation has come; the old has gone, the new is here!

E very muscle, joint and tendon in my body clicked as I awoke from my coma; the beeping of the machines I was connected to got louder, I slowly opened my eyes and blinked a few times before everything came back into focus. The familiar antiseptic smell, the scurry of footsteps just outside of nurses rushing up and down the corridors of the ward; I was officially back on earth, making a rather underwhelming entrance at Durbanville Mediclinic.

"Oh no," I muttered, "I'm back..."

I felt so groggy, the reality of being back in my human state hit me like a punch in the stomach. The memories of the extraordinary experiences of heaven were still vivid in my mind, and thoughts of my daughter Gillian made my heart ached with every beat. I missed her so much that I would've traded the whole world just to be with her, but at the same time I was so grateful for the grace and mercy Jesus bestowed upon me.

"Gideon!" My Mother's voice reverberated throughout the ward. "My darling son, you're awake!"

She was walking in with a coffee, and she dropped it with a messy thud just before the nurses rushed in. They immediately checked my vital signs and did all the necessary things to make sure I was responsive and well. Once they had given my mother the all clear, she showered me with kisses and the kind of affection that she was no doubt reserving for a grandchild.

"Gideon," she said grabbing my face with both her hands. "You still remember me right?"

"How could I forget, Mom?" I smiled at her, much to her relief.

"This is a miracle!" She shouted. "Thank you Jesus!"

My Doctor came in soon afterwards, his trademark stethoscope swinging around his neck, thick-rimmed glasses and greying hair. He had a look of utter amazement on his face, I could tell he had given up hope of my recovery.

"You're a living miracle Mr Daniels," He said, scrutinizing the charts at my bedside.

"How long was I in a coma for?"

"Thirty-two days," he said, I could still hear the disbelief in his voice. "Nothing medically was pointing to your recovery at this point, you're a very lucky young man."

"I'm not lucky Dr Nigel," I replied. "I'm blessed because I serve an Almighty God."

"We will keep you here under observation for the next three d ays," he replied after a short pause, he smiled and turned to the nurse. "Move him to the general ward."

"Gideon, are you hungry?" True to form, my mother's first question was about food, and I realized that I missed her much more than I thought.

"I'm fine mom, thanks." I smiled, "thank you for being here, and for never giving up on me."

"I never stopped praying for you..." She grabbed my hand.

For the first time in my life, I listened not to respond but to understand my mother, where she came from, what made her, shaped her, what conditioned her thoughts. I gave her all my undivided attention, and let her speak her heart out. Before, within minutes, my mind would go in every other direction that life was pulling me, and

I would give her quick one word replies just to end the conversation abruptly so I could move on. Now I was with her, completely in the moment, one thing I learnt in heaven was the value of each moment, because life can change in an instant; and if we miss it then it won't return. Life really is too short to waste on things that pull us away from where God wants us to be, one moment at a time, one day at a time. I needed to be in this moment with my mother, so that through listening to her talk, and acknowledging her loneliness, I could be the instrument that God uses to show her that he cherishes her every word.

"What happened to you?" My Mother asked, frowning.

"What do you mean?" I replied.

"You're different," she said, "Is it the drugs?"

"I hope not," I laughed. Then took a deep breath, wondering if my Mother was ready for my response? "Let's just say I lost the world, but found my soul."

"You can trust me," she looked me in the eye, and I could tell she was expecting me to tell her something extraordinary. "I know something out of this world happened to you while you were away and I want to hear it."

I shared my experience of heaven with her in great detail, how everything looked, how spectacular the food tasted, how amazing it was to have met Jesus and Mother Mary, as well as some of the saints. I told her about dad, Natalie and of course Gillian. By the end of my story, we were both moved to tears. I was going through mixed emotions, my soul was yearning to be back in heaven with my heavenly family, but my spirit was ignited with purpose as I shared the incredible story of heaven and my experience with Jesus Christ. My whole existence suddenly gained new meaning, by losing all earthly significance; I was braving completely new territory and had nothing but my faith to lean on, this scared but exhilarated me all at the same time.

"I'm speechless..." My mother said, wiping away tears.

"Mom," I grabbed her hand and squeezed it tightly. "Heaven is real, and nothing on earth compares to it. I promise you."

"I believe you," she smiled. "Oh how I long to be with your father."

"Just keep praying and know that Jesus has prepared a place for all of us there," I said, "it's up to us to keep hold of his hand in this life, so we don't lose our place with him in the next."

I was discharged from the hospital three days later, my mom insisted that I stay with her until I was strong enough to live on my own. Besides being a woman, and my mom, I was in no position to argue, considering I had technically been dead for a while. I hadn't been back home in ten years, so the trip back to Paarl was a strange one filled with all sorts of conflicting emotions; it's like I was going back in time, Gideon Daniels: take two? The strangeness of the car ride back to Paarl was exacerbated by my mom's off-tune voice singing along to Dolly Parton's greatest hits. I couldn't help but laugh at the beautiful absurdity of it all.

Not much had changed; my mom still had too much parsley growing in between her flowers and ferns, she still hadn't gotten round to fixing the crack in the window that I had accidently caused by playing cricket with the neighbourhood kids in our garden, our front door still creaked so loud that it notified the entire neighbourhood that we had arrived. Back then I had dreams of playing for the Proteas, it's sad how things change so fast, sadder how other things stay exactly the same and the saddest is when both scenarios play out due to things that are beyond our control. It occurred to me how being back on earth meant I was once again susceptible to the impending sense of failure that ultimately hinders every human being from time to time. I was coming face to face with my past, not just in my thoughts this time, there was no running, I had to confront it and give it all I had, no matter how inadequate I thought my all was.

"Hey buddy!" Our family dog came rushing through the corridor and jumped onto me, licking my hands and face. He was a little slower than I last remember, a little fatter too, but still had the same incredible enthusiasm I had missed him so much.

The house still had that distinct smell of spices and eucalyptus, for me that was the smell that made me call this house, home. I felt so removed and yet connected to this place at the same time. Part of me wishes I had never left, but most of me wishes I could just come back and start over, give me a chance to make better choices. Nostalgia is a double-edged sword, it takes us back to happier times but cuts us with the reality that those moments will forever be encased behind the glass of our memories, where we will forever see them but never touch them again. While moving through the house, I was struck by memories; my fifth birthday when my mom made a teddy-bear shaped cake, the first Christmas I remember was when I had turned seven, and got a video game console for Christmas, my first kiss was under the orange tree in our backyard, we were fifteen and after playing truth, dare or command; I was commanded to kiss Miranda, the girl who was constantly mocking me for my weird hairstyle and walking impediment due to having flat feet. She kissed me back because she knew how much I would hate it. I often thought about my life, and wondered how it would've turned out if I had never met Lillian. It's useless to dwell in the past, but regret had always chained me to it, and this regret was as deeply embedded in me as the marrow in my bones.

"You can go settle in," my mom said, interrupting my thoughts, "I've changed the linens on your bed."

My room was just as I had last remembered it; my favourite movie posters still adorned the wall. I moved out when I was 19, two years after I met Lillian and we moved in together. So my teen years were still alive and well in here. So strange to walk into a place knowing that so much has changed, and yet some parts still remained exactly the same fifteen years later. My mom had left things exactly as they were; sometimes I wish that's what I had done too. I opened one of the drawers on my side table, and found photo albums.

I also found a diary with bad poetry I had written about how bleak life was through the lens of puberty and teenage angst that never truly left me if I must be honest with myself. Looking at all the old photographs of me, I noticed how I had exchanged my hair for some added weight, most people look at their past for the mistakes they've made. I looked at my past with regret because of the mistakes I was too afraid to make. I realized for the first time the core of my infinite melancholy... I had lived the past decade of my life in complete irony. Living my life in a past that like a thick fog, was tangible, heavy and full of times I had gotten lost in; but ultimately it was times I would never get back, times that just like thick fog, eventually dissipated and would leave me alone on the road of life, not knowing what direction to take. What I had lost that was so much more important than my hair, was my hope for a better life.

"I have not forsaken you, so don't forsake me..."

I felt those words echo in my heart, and recognized the voice instantly. Looking around the room in surprise, I put the relics of my past back in the drawer and slammed it shut. Jesus was with me, it was his voice I heard, I knew it and could feel it deep in my spirit. I rushed over to my cupboard as a wholly different memory from my past came to mind. I was seven years old, it was my First Holy Communion; I remember how my mother had bought a white suit for the occasion, I had no idea what all the fuss was about back then, but I was just happy to be dressed in nice clothes and to be spending the day with my friends, enjoying all the good food.

"Here you go... may he carry you all the days of your life," my mother said, handing me a gift.

The box was wrapped in blue paper with angels on it, I of course was hoping it was a video game, but expected a box of chocolates. I hadn't really taken note of my mom's words because I was too excited about the gift. I was wrong on both counts, once I had ripped through the wrapping paper, what I found was a Bible. A King James Bible with beautiful silver pages, I thanked my mother with a hug and a kiss, then rushed off to my room, where I had tossed the Bible at the back of my cupboard...

Now I stood before my cupboard 28 years later, I opened it, rummaged through my clothes and found the gift my mother gave me for my First Holy Communion, just where I had left it. My King James Bible, still in its box covered by dust; I blew off the dust, and opened it again for only the second time in my life. The silver pages still sparkled in the sunlight coming in through the window.

"Lord," I said, looking out the window at the blue sky overhead, stretching out endlessly like my longing for something I still hadn't quite grasped. "I wish I just could've stayed in heaven with you, you know how terrible I am at life in this world, why oh why did you send me back here?"

Flipping through the pages, I closed my eyes and asked God for an answer. I stopped to read the first verse that caught my eye:

John 14:8
"I will not leave you as orphans; I will come to you."
I FELL BACK ON MY BED, and just kept reading that line over and over, until tears filled my eyes and I cried quietly, in peace with tears running down either side of my face, until I fell into a deep sleep.

Chapter Fifteen

Proverbs 16:9
A man's heart plans his way, but the Lord directs his steps.

Physiotherapy had been long and arduous, but progress was made, I had regained my strength and was ready to go back to work; only to get a letter from my employers that the company had liquidated, and I would be getting my final payment at the end of the month. My life had all of a sudden become that Alanis Morrisette song. I had been keeping up the rent of my flat in Bellville with the payment of my accumulated sick leave from the company, and I had put off going back home partly because of my recovery but mostly because I was afraid. I was in such a great place spiritually right now, I had gone to heaven! Was revisiting the flat such a good idea? I didn't think so. I didn't want to risk losing whatever progress I had made. But now that I was unemployed, going back home was inevitable. I would have to go back and get my things.

My Mom was insisting on driving with me back to my flat so I could go pick up my things and return the keys to the landlord. I'm pretty sure she just wanted to make sure I wouldn't skip lunch, and also to try and convince me to burn everything I had that ever belonged to Lillian, they were not very close, to put it politely. Lillian said my mom was always meddling in our life, my Mom said Lillian didn't love me for who I was, but for who she wanted to turn me into. When all was said and done, it was my mother who was there and not Lillian, so I can't disagree with her. If Lillian truly loved me, my mother wouldn't have been an issue, no matter what.

"Mom," I said, grabbing her shoulders and looking into her green eyes that showed me a thousand stories I never took the time to listen to. "I need to do this... alone. I will stop for a bite to eat. I promise." I winked at her and grabbed the car keys.

"Please be careful," she pleaded with me so intensely that it reminded me of that scene in the movie Armageddon when they were about to enter the rocket and were saying goodbye to their loved ones.

"Mom," I kissed her forehead. "I'll be fine."

It was a bright sunny day in Paarl, and the temperature was giving me a reason to crank up the air conditioner. I rummaged through my mom's CD collection in the hopes that I would find something decent to keep me company; I settled on John Mayer, which was actually my CD and I was convinced Lillian had taken with her when she moved out. So there I was driving back to my old life, being serenaded by John Mayer singing about how he was waiting on the world to change, how I related to this song was insane right now. It had been four months since I was last home, other than added dust, everything was exactly as I had left it. It's like I was reliving the day I attempted suicide, in a weird way, Jesus had brought me back to the day I wanted everything to end, just so I could start over; it's like I was living some kind of pseudo-spiritual Groundhog Day. Walking through my flat brought back some unforgettable memories, like the night I decided to surprise Lillian by cooking dinner for the first time and almost burnt down the kitchen, we ended up eating out and spending the night at a hotel; others not so good, like the endless fights we would have about me not being extroverted enough, or not really concerned with how I dressed or looked, which embarrassed and infuriated her in equal measure.

I loved Lillian with every fibre of my being, I gave her my all and when I saw that wasn't enough, I tried to give her whatever else she wanted, completely losing who I was in the process. It took years, but I finally realized that Lillian never loved me; she loved the idea that she had of me in her head. She spent our entire relationship trying to change me into the man she truly loved, only to realize that you can camouflage a person's appearance, but you can't change who they are on the inside. Lillian was my first love, but me... I was just her rebound, her ticket to get out of the painful life she was forced to live when her previous relationship ended. I wasn't good enough for her, who I was trying to be for her wasn't good enough for her, and after seven years of trying, I was just replaced like some kind of cog in the great big machine that was her dream life... a life she had gone on to live, leaving me behind to pick up the pieces, trapped in the memories of the life we were supposed to have lived together, and that's just too much war for one person to make peace with in one lifetime.

I walked through the corridor, and looked at all the photographs hanging on the walls, relics of every Christmas, Valentine's Day and birthday; like a museum dedicated to the historical part of my life I couldn't seem to escape. My heart was bursting at the seams with memories of a life lived and simultaneously unlived, so far my only escape had been my experience in heaven, and ironically even heaven escaped me in that sense. So in light of all this, I did what most people do when they find themselves at the edge of the abyss of heartache, buried myself in work by grabbing the empty boxes I had brought with me and started packing away all my things room by room, leaving my bedroom for last. I had made an agreement with the landlord that he could keep my furniture in exchange for any repairs that needed to be done to the place. The faint scent of cologne and deodorant was in the air of my bedroom; much has been said about how to measure a person's character; some say it can be measured according to their playlist, others say their diet, but for me I think much can be said about a person by what books they read. Judging from The Great Gatsby and My Uncle Oswald, to Silver linings Playbook and High Fidelity; I guess it would be safe to say from my book collection, that I'm an incurable dreamer wrapped up in a life of missed opportunities and failures. Emptying out my bedside table, I stumbled upon a picture that made my whole world stop in that moment. It was our first 3D scan of Gillian, I couldn't be there because I was stuck at work, which made me feel like the worst husband and father in the world. The message Lillian left me on the back of that picture brought back all the heartbreak: *"Babe, no matter what we've done wrong, she will always make it right. love you. Xox."* Suddenly I remembered why I wanted to die. The only good thing that happened to me was taken away, and the rest I either let slip through my fingers or had paused long enough to feel it's breath on my skin before watching it pass me by.

People say we make our own happiness, but I don't agree with that. I've seen people with far less than me enjoying a much more fulfilled life, while those with tons more, feel equally miserable or more so. If joy was a man-made construct, we'd all be happy in our own way. But that's not the case, isn't that an indication that true joy can only be found outside of ourselves and our capabilities? My trip to heaven proves that... or am I wrong? Either way, I'm stuck, living this life, regretting some of the times I said yes and wondering what life would've looked like if I had said no.

"Jesus!" I shouted, looking up at the ceiling. "I miss Gillian! I've lost my wife, I've lost my child, and now I've lost my job! I had you when I was in heaven, why did you send me back here!?"

I broke down, clutching the 3D scan to my chest for an undetermined amount of time. All I wanted to do was be back in heaven and hold Gillian in my arms for the rest of my life. I eventually composed myself and finished packing up my things into boxes. Once I was done, drove away, knowing that I had just lost a part of my heart that I was never going to get back...

ON MY WAY BACK HOME, I drove past a church and noticed the door was open. I hadn't been to church in a while, and if I was going to talk anyone, I figured one of God's official servants that didn't know me would be a good bet. I walked in and the smell of incense and candles welcomed me, I looked up at the crucifix on the wall high above my head and closed my eyes. For those brief moments, with that wonderful fragrance, I was back in heaven; walking the gardens, feeling the utter joy and holding my daughter in my arms. I needed to pray. So I walked to the front of the church and knelt down in one of the pews.

"Jesus," I said, "I miss my little girl, I don't know what to do here. Please, I need your help. You said I must call on you. I'm calling now. Please help me. Amen."

"You new here, son?"

I looked over my shoulder and saw a priest walking from the back of the church towards me.

"Just passing through Father," I replied.

"Do you mind?" He asked, gesturing to take a seat next to me.

"Not at all Father," I said, "this is after all your church."

He sat next to me, he had a gentle face and his black hair had shades of grey that matched perfectly to the white collar and black shirt of his priestly uniform.

"From my experience," he said, "people who come to God's house outside of mass times are looking for answers that the world hasn't been able to give them... Father Gary," he stretched out his hand.

"Gideon Daniels," I shook his hand, and after a short pause. "How many year's experience are we talking here?"

"I've been a priest for ten years," he smiled. "I'm assuming you're Catholic?"

"I don't really know what I am right now."

"Sounds like you need a listening ear and a broad shoulder," he replied. "May I volunteer?"

What I thought was going to be a quick visit, turned into a two hour conversation to a complete stranger who happened to be a priest. I grew up always wanting to be the tough guy, the one who could walk everything off, in every sense of the word. None of that was true though, losing Lillian and Gillian was enough to completely destroy me, now that I saw Gillian, not being with her was destroying me all over again. I had to face it, losing Lillian was something I was never going to get over either and I didn't know what to do about it.

"I get that God called you to be a priest and all that," I said, "but have you ever wondered what your life would be like if you had made different choices? Don't you ever regret becoming a priest? It seems like such a solitary life... or are you going to give me one of those cliché spiritual tic-tacs like "I'm perfectly happy because I'm working for the Lord?"

"Ah Gideon," Father Gary laughed, "I'm human, just as susceptible to all the things that make us doubt ourselves and our lives as you. Do I regret I becoming a priest? No, never." His eyes suddenly became distant. "Do I ever wonder what my life would be like if I had made different choices? More times than I would like to admit."

"But are you happy?" I asked.

"Happiness is fleeting," he replied. "Do we as human beings even know what happiness is? I mean, one day we want burgers, then the next we want soup. In summer, we complain that it's too hot, yet when its winter, we're crying about the cold. If I had gotten married, part of me would always wonder what life would've been like as a priest; also, I would've been constantly worried about my kids, the insecurities of being a good father and a good husband would always make me wonder if my wife would love me forever. Not to say I am completely worry free as a priest... I always second guess myself after a sermon, always worry about whether I've helped my parishioners when they reach out to me. But at least as a priest, I don't have to do it all in my own strength. Families shouldn't have to do it all in their own strength either. Speaking of a family, each time I baptize a baby, I partake in the parent's joy, each time I do a funeral, I share in the pain of the loved ones... My parishioners are my family. I'm alone a lot, but far from lonely."

"Go on?" Gideon looked at the empty pews around him, and couldn't fathom how this man had no one but an empty church for company, and was still content.

"Gideon," he tapped my shoulder. "God calls each one of us to a specific purpose in this life, but he also gave us freewill to choose what path we want to take. No matter what we choose, it will always be at the expense of something else and everything has pros and cons," he pointed up. "God watches over us like a worried father, loving us no matter what we choose, hoping that we include him in our decisions, so he can help us when we fall and guide us when we're lost. That's why Jesus became one of us, to take on our fickle willpower and vulnerabilities, so he could conquer them for us. Jesus is our true north Gideon, all he wants to do is lead us back to our eternal home, where he's already prepared a place for each one of us." He had this immensely satisfied look on his face, like a man who had just retired and knew that he was about to reap the benefits of a life well lived.

"No matter how I feel, I find peace knowing that I am doing God's work, and that each setback is just another stepping stone that takes me closer to that place Jesus prepared for me. Gideon... thank you for sharing a little bit of your story with me, no matter where you go, or what you do, just remember to keep holding Jesus's Hand. He will lead you through the dark, carry you through every storm, wipe away every tear when you're sad and laugh with you in every joy. Things will always change, and as human beings no matter how strong we want to make ourselves out to be, change will always be difficult, and sometimes it will knock us to the ground, Jesus himself fell three times while carrying his cross. But each time, he just got up and kept going. That's why he is the way, the truth and the life... no matter what happens, or what you do, just keep holding Jesus's hand, and that will guarantee that his peace remains in your heart, and after ten years. I can honestly say, that is better than all the fleeting moments of happiness the world can give put together." He looked me in the eye and smiled. "Well, I have to get ready for mass... you're welcome to stay?"

"Thank you Father Gary, but I should be heading back home..."

"God bless you Gideon, in all you do."

Chapter Sixteen

Matthew 7:24
"Therefore whoever hears these words of mine and puts them into practice
is like a wise man who builds his house on the rock."

I spent the entire week looking for a new job, going door to door handing out CV's, trawling the internet for job ads. Losing a job because of stupidity, like that one job I lost because I forgot to put up the wet floor sign when I was mopping and in walked my manager and slipped is one thing. But losing a job for reasons that was beyond my control made me feel utterly useless.

"Any luck?" My mom asked, flipping some French toast in a pan.

"Nothing yet," I sighed. "I know I mustn't be picky, but I would like a job that's going to make me want to get up every morning at least."

"Well, have you prayed about it?" My mom went straight for the jugular, as she piled French toast onto my plate.

"Cleary not enough," I replied, thanking her for the breakfast.

"When we go to mass," she said, taking a bite of her toast, "we'll ask Jesus to open the right door for you."

"Sounds like a plan," I replied.

I hadn't been to church in about ten years, I grew up Catholic and my mother was a typical Catholic mom, she had raised me with a sandal in one hand and rosary beads in the other. Throughout my childhood and much of my teen years, I only came to mass because I was told to. I had no interest in what the Priest was saying, or what was happening on the altar because I was too busy either looking around for the prettiest girl in the pews, or thinking about what I was going to have for lunch, anything really except the reason why we were all gathered there; to visit our creator. Today was going to be different though, I could feel it deep in my heart.

Paarl Catholic Church was just as I had last remembered it; the wooden finishes of the tabernacle, the statues with the outline colours fading and the unvarnished pews just added to the rustic feel of the place of worship. The distinct smell of melted wax from the candles and incense just filled me with a sense of peace now that I struggled to find anywhere else. This was Jesus's home on earth, and for the first time in my life, I realized that here, I could be exactly who I was without fear.

"Where's Father Patrick?" I asked, not recognizing the priest who was making his way up to the altar.

"He retired two years ago," my mother whispered in my ear. "This is Father Brendan."

He wasn't much older than me, mid to late forties I guessed, his hairline was receding and his hair was greying, but the skin on his face was smooth, and the look in his eyes reflected that same curious joy that I saw in the eyes of Father Gary when I had spoken to him earlier. I didn't want to become a priest, but I desperately wanted that same joy they seemed to have.

I'd heard many stories of people who said that God had spoken to them, either through signs or some even claimed to have heard him speak into their hearts. I'd gone to heaven and met Jesus personally, so I had no doubt in my mind that He was real, but I had never had an encounter with him on earth, and I was finding the ability to connect with him virtually impossible right now. I had lost my wife, my daughter, now my job, and just couldn't figure out why Jesus had sent me back here. Why couldn't I have just stayed with him? What purpose did I serve here, if everything I touched eventually slipped through my fingers? "Jesus, please, what am I doing here, seriously? I don't know what you want from me? Tell me what to do, or please take me back to heaven, I'm lost here." I said to myself, and then I heard the gospel for the day...

"Matthew 7:24..." Father Brendan said.

Father Brendan's homily was one of those hard-hitting ones that I could tell was going to stay with me for the rest of my life. I could feel my heart burn within me as he spoke:

"Show of hands, who here has built something? Even if it was just assembling a table they bought from Game... just for today, we'll call that building," He smiled, and people were putting up their hands while erupting into laughter. "Great, now I know who to call." Father Brendan laughed. "Now, how many of you built that item or structure without reading the instructions?" He paused for a moment, and after noticing that no one was putting up their hands, he nodded. "Good, that shows you are wise." He paced around the altar slowly, making sure he had everyone's attention. "Imagine watching a game of football where none of the players obeyed the rules, it would be complete chaos right?" People nodded in agreement. "I'm pretty sure there would be quite a few serious injuries too. Can you imagine building a house without following the usual procedure of laying a good, solid foundation? The house would most definitely collapse and most likely kill everyone inside it." I could tell everyone was paying attention. "Rules are not there to restrict us but to protect us from harm. When Jesus says that if we take heed of his words and put them into practice we will be like wise men who built their houses on the rock; he's not only saying that we will be kept safe from the storms and dangers of life, but he's also giving us instructions on how to store up treasures for ourselves in heaven. My brothers and sisters in Christ, maybe you haven't heard Jesus speak to you audibly, but that's because we shouldn't be listening to Jesus with our physical ears, Jesus gave us the Holy Spirit, to enable us to listen to him with our hearts... And if we ever hope to connect with him all the way there in heaven, then the best way to do it, just like with anything else we want to learn... we have to read the manual." He picked up his Bible. "Let's all be wise family, and learn how to listen to him with our hearts by reading his word and asking the Holy Spirit to open us up to him."

I knew clapping in church would be inappropriate, so I contained myself, but the message that Father Brendan shared with us was incredible, and for reasons that I just couldn't explain, it was exactly what I needed to hear. It made sense, because ever since my experience in heaven, I was constantly focusing on hearing Jesus on a physical level, almost like I was expecting to hear from him with my ears, instead of trying to listen to him with my heart. From that moment, I just closed my eyes and said a little prayer, and literally asked Jesus to fill me with the Holy Spirit and help me open my heart, so I could connect with him again and get the guidance I needed. I remember learning in catechism as a kid about the Eucharist and how by the outpouring of the Holy Spirit, the bread and wine transform into the body and blood of Jesus Christ and how on a spiritual level, we actually consume Jesus' very presence, as per the words of the gospel of John 6:54; so when I went up for Communion, I really focused on surrendering my heart to the Lord to the best of my ability.

Just before the final blessing, Father Brendan asked us to remain seated to hear the announcements for the week, and he said there was going to be a special announcement by a lady named Claire. She was a young lady, early to mid-twenties I assumed, short, red hair, green eyes, she had a gentle voice, the kind that you want to hear when you need someone to talk to.

"I am qualified nurse and for the past two years, I've been running the Bethlehem Hospice of Paarl that provides more affordable treatment to people who are terminally ill or cannot afford to go to a hospital, and don't want to have their loved ones alone at home. It hasn't been an easy journey, but by God's grace, we've managed to get by and helped over 100 patients at our facility, most have passed on, but with the dignity they deserve. I pride myself in saying that we provide more than just medical care for the body, but spiritual care for the soul. So, we are looking for an admin clerk because Margaret, who has been our admin clerk from day one has retired and decided to move to Laangebaan. So we need someone to fill in her spot, if you are interested, you can come and see me after mass. Thank you. God bless."

My mother did an awful job of subtly getting my attention by nudging me in ribs much harder than necessary. "You must go see her about that job, this is the door Jesus is opening for you?"

"To be around people who are dying every day," I shrugged, rubbing the area of my ribs that would surely bruise thanks to my mom's incessant nudging.

"You get to be around Claire all day long, isn't that enough incentive?" She smiled.

"Mom," I laughed.

Claire was definitely attractive, but apart from her being too young for me, given my luck with dating ever since the divorce, she was obviously spoken for. Besides, I needed a job, not a girlfriend. My mom was right about one thing, I had prayed for Jesus to open a door, and he didn't make me wait very long. I truly believed this was Him opening a door for me. So I was going to go speak to Claire and get more info on her job offer.

"Hi Claire," I approached her. "My name is Gideon, and I've come to find out a little bit more about that job you mentioned?"

"Pleased to meet you Gideon," she said with a warm smile, shaking my hand. "I wasn't expecting a man to show interest, so I have to be honest, we're a small operation, so the salary isn't great."

"I don't have plans to become a millionaire," I smiled.

"Good to know," she laughed.

"I just need a job right now, and as crazy as this may sound," I replied, "I truly believe this job is God's way of answering my prayers. So what do you need from me?"

"I can understand that," she smiled. "God does work in mysterious ways as they say, well I would need a CV of course and we'll take it from there? Here's my contacts."

"Of course," I replied, taking her card. "I will send it to you today."

"Hello Mrs Claire," My mom approached us just as I was about to walk away.

.

"It's Miss, but let's stick to Claire please," she smiled.

Smooth mom... Smooth. I knew exactly what she was trying to do.

"I'm Gideon's mom, I guarantee you, you won't find a more qualified person to work with."

"Ok mom, I think we better get going..."

"I don't doubt that ma'am," she laughed.

"Sorry..." I whispered behind my mom's back.

Claire gave me a thumbs up and off we went, I was in good spirits and quite amazed that Jesus had literally answered my prayers in such a short space of time.

THREE DAYS LATER, CLAIRE sent me an email to tell me that I had been given the job and could start immediately. My mom's level of excitement was equivalent to the time she found out she was going to become a grandmother, Claire and I were going to get married and have ten children already, I could see it in her eyes; despite me explaining to her that Claire was much too young for me, and no doubt had a boyfriend already.

"Age is just a number Gideon," my mom said, "look at your grandfather, he was 12 years older than your grandmother."

"Mom," I replied. "Back then divorce was a capital crime punishable by execution. You could be married to Hitler and would need to stay with him for life. Times have changed."

"But God has not," she replied, "age really is just a number dear." She straightened my collar for me. "Love always conquers all obstacles, now go out there and impress." She kissed me on the cheek.

"Thanks Mom," I smiled, "see you later."

My mom was right about love always conquering, but it's got to be reciprocated otherwise all it causes is pain. Even with Jesus, He loved each person on earth enough to die in our place, but we need to respond to that love, otherwise our salvation remains incomplete. I pulled up the driveway of this house with a blue sign hanging loosely above the entrance gate: *Bethlehem Hospice of Paarl*. I knocked on the front door, and an older gentleman answered.

"Hi," I said, "I'm looking for Claire?"

"Come on in," he said, "you must be the new guy."

"Yes I am."

"Frank," he stretched out his hand. "I'm the handy man."

"Gideon, pleased to meet you," I shook his hand.

"Hi Gideon," Claire walked in from another room with an armful of files.

She dropped the files on a desk, came to greet me and welcomed me before giving me a quick tour of the place. The place was small and needed some work because the paint was fading in some of the rooms, parts of the ceiling had water damage, but the patient's living areas were in top shape though. Clearly their budget was prioritized correctly. They had everything that they needed to do what they do best, take care of people.

"Sorry things are a little crazy," Claire said, leading the way as we moved through the facility.

"How many patients have you got here at the moment?"

"Twenty," she replied. "three of them are children, and the rest are elderly, unfortunately in the final stages of their respective illnesses. All palliative care."

"Doesn't it depress you at times?"

"Sometimes I get sad," she sighed. "But I know I am doing a great service for God's kingdom by preparing these people for heaven. Gideon, I meant what I said in church, we're so much more than just a hospice, here we do our best to take care of people's souls." She looked at her watch. "Listen Gideon, I'm so sorry for kind of throwing you in the deep end here. I promise to do a formal introduction in the coming days and introduce you to the rest of the team and the patients, but for now, I really need you to please grab those files I dumped on that table in there and work on them for me please?"

"Of course, what are they?"

"They are our supplier folders, and I need you to please sort them out and go through the invoices to see what's still outstanding and what's not please?"

"Sure thing."

"Oh..." She was just about to rush out, and then turned to face me again. "Can you please create new spread sheets for our suppliers and just modernize our system a little please? I loved Margaret to bits, but she was quite old school and not really into the new ways of admin clerking."

"Ai, ai captain," I replied, immediately regretting the words as they came out of my mouth.

"Thank you," she smiled and rushed off.

Chapter Seventeen

Matthew 18:3
And he said: "Truly I tell you, unless you change and become like little
children, you will never enter the kingdom of heaven.

Catching up on the backlog took some time, but I had managed to sort everything out and come up with a more digital approach to keep their admin up to date. I had also taken charge of the orders and payments, which definitely played into my skillset. I had met some of the patients, and Claire had managed to introduce me to the rest of the team, we always started and ended the day with prayer... and doughnuts with coffee. Definitely a highlight of each working day for me, both the doughnuts and coffee, as well as the prayers; I loved praying, it was the one time I could just pour my heart out to God, knowing that there wouldn't be sarcastic remarks, or pleasant sound bites to try and make me radically change who I was. God was always ready to listen, when I needed to talk, and I cherished those moments.

"Hi Gideon," Claire said, her perfume filled the air, so I knew it was her before responding to her greeting. "I've been promising to introduce you to our children here, the day has finally arrived. Can you break away for a little bit?"

"Of course," I replied.

"You've been doing a great job, thank you so much," Claire said.

"Happy to be making a difference," I replied, following her into the garden.

Mr Van Zyl and Mrs Morake were sitting opposite each other between a chess board, arguing about whose turn it was to make the next move, they both swore like sailors, it was really entertaining and I couldn't help but laugh and have a bursting amount of affection and pity for these two soldiers that had ran the race of life. I totally understood why Claire's passion was within these walls. There's this overwhelming perception that when people grow old, they've run their course so to speak, they are insignificant because their contribution to the world is past the sell by date. This couldn't be further from the truth, the elderly are way ahead of the rest of us on the race of life, because they've already arrived where we're still planning to go.

"And now the kids," Claire said, she had a sparkle in her eye, I could tell these children had a very special place in her heart. She opened the door to a play area on the opposite side of the garden.

"This is Tumelo, Jared and our little girl here is Victoria," Claire said, introducing them one by one, as they came running towards us.

I hugged each of them and had a brief chat with each one, asking them the usual things we ask kids, like what their favourite colour is, and what games they were playing. Being with these kids was reminding me of Gillian, that's probably why I was particularly drawn to Victoria; she was the oldest of them at eight years old, her favourite colour was purple like Barney the dinosaur, and she loved jumping on a trampoline. She had a headscarf, and her face was gaunt from what I assumed was her illness, but she had big brown eyes that hadn't lost the infinite sparkle of childhood joy and innocence.

Being with Victoria made me miss Gillian, but it also gave my days that extra sparkle, because in a strange way I got to be with Gillian again through Victoria, answering all her million questions, and just watching her be a kid.

"Why are they here?" I asked Claire, having a cup of coffee with her, as we both looked out of the window at the kids.

"Tumelo has a brain tumour, Jared a heart condition and Victoria has a cancer that requires a bone marrow transplant," Claire replied, taking a deep breath. "Tumelo and Jared's parents are going to come and collect them by the end of the month because their respective doctors have already found alternative treatments for them, and Victoria's parents went to America, because they are planning to move there by the end of the year, so they went ahead to set up treatment and try get a suitable donor there in case they don't get one here."

"That's awful," I said, I felt I had just been stabbed right in the heart. "They're so young! Why?"

"God works in mysterious ways Gideon," Claire responded, and put her hand on my shoulder. "We can never lose hope."

"I know... it's just hard when it's kids you know."

"You've taken a real liking to Vicky," Claire said. "She's adorable of course and anyone would fall absolutely in love with her, but you seem to have a special connection to her."

"Let's just say she reminds me of someone..."

"I'd love to hear about that person some time," she smiled, and finished her coffee. "I've got to run, chat later."

Despite my best efforts, which included reading my TV's instruction manual, I couldn't sleep. I spent hours tossing and turning, because I couldn't get Victoria out of my mind. I couldn't help but think of the anguish her parents must be going through at the fear of losing their little girl, it's an anguish I knew all too well.

"I've got to try and help her," I said rubbing my eyes for the umpteenth time of the night. I looked at my bedside digital clock. 3 am, I turned to face the window and eventually dozed off to sound of crickets chirping outside and fluctuating thoughts of Victoria getting her bone marrow transplant and me getting reunited with Gillian.

"MORNING CLAIRE," I walked into her office, but noticed how distant she was. "Claire?"

"Oh hi Gideon," she replied.

"Are you okay?"

"Yes, sorry," she replied. "Just got a lot of paperwork to get through."

Claire was lying, I had been lied to enough times to recognize when someone was omitting the truth. Not that she was obliged to tell me anything, but I was just making an observation.

"Did you want to talk to me about something?"

"I want to take the test and see if I'm a match for Victoria?"

"Really?" She smiled.

"Absolutely, I want to help her in any way I can," I replied.

"That's beautiful..." She said, smiling. "It's amazing to see there are still good people in the world."

"Only God is truly good Claire," I replied.

"Sometimes I have my doubts, to be honest..."

"I'd love to hear about them sometime?" I replied, remembering her words to me.

"I'll get you the doctor's number," she smiled, and rummaged through her drawers before pulling out his card for me.

"Thank you," I said, "hey Claire, what are the chances that I could take Vicky out for ice cream sometime? She has no family here at the moment, I just want to do something nice for her."

"That should be ok, but I will need to get the all clear from her parents, next time they call I will ask. Provided you go with one of the nurses, that should be fine though, I will let you know."

I HATED HOSPITALS, they were like the explicit version of airports, which I didn't really like either. Actually what I hate is goodbyes, both hospitals and airports are breeding grounds for them. The only difference is that at airports, people come dressed up in their best outfits for a holiday or move they've been planning for months or years; in hospitals, people don't have time to plan, they just arrive at this unplanned destination, naked, very vulnerable... and never ready to say goodbye. I knew what it felt like to lose a child, if I could stop someone else from being afflicted with the great chasm caused by that pain. I was going to do it.

"Mr Daniels," Dr Lee's nurse called, flipping through a file. "Follow me."

Needles didn't rank very high on my list of favourite pass times, so at the moment of truth, I just turned my head and closed my eyes, imagining myself walking on the beach as the sting of the syringe tearing through my skin rippled throughout my left arm.

"We'll have the results for you in a week or two," the nurse said, filling out the rest of my details. "Thank you for availing yourself for Vicky."

"I just hope it's not in vain."

Claire told me that Vicky's parents were ok with the idea, as long as we take all the necessary precautions of course, and gave me the day off to take Vicky out as I had requested. The condition was that we were accompanied by Nurse Edna, who was all too happy to join us. My heart was full, as I prepared for the day, by preparing a basket of sandwiches and I even went out and bought a children's music CD, it was the soundtrack to some movie called Frozen, definitely not my type of music, but I imagined that if Gillian were with me, this is what she would've loved too.

"Gideon," my mom said, helping me with the basket. "Please don't replace Gillian in your heart with this little girl Vicky?"

"What?" Her question left me a little unsettled. "That's ridiculous."

"Gideon," she continued, "Only God knows if Vicky is going to recover, I just don't want you to get hurt again, and remember she is not your daughter. She's not Gillian…"

"I know that mom!" I was so much angrier than I wanted to be. "Gillian is irreplaceable! No one will ever replace her! That's not what I am doing with Vicky, and she's not going to die!"

"Ok…" She grabbed my hands. "Calm down."

"I'm sorry..."

"I just don't want to see you that broken again, that's all."

"Thanks Mom," I gave her a hug. "I'm just trying to be there for Vicky, because she's got no one."

"God bless you for that."

On the drive to work, I thought about what my mom said, was I really replacing Gillian with Vicky on some unconscious level? I couldn't explain it, but I was so drawn to her, I loved her enough, that I could almost say she was my own child, and the thought of her dying scared me to no end.

"Are you ready to go Vicky?" Nurse Edna said, grabbing Vicky's bag.

"Yes, she came out and ran with all the strength she could muster into my arms.

I picked her up and carried her to my car. Her face was so pale, like a ghost's from one of those horror movies I could never finish watching. But her eyes were alight with the excitement of knowing that she was going to leave the disinfected confines of the clinic that was her life, and I felt so privileged to be the one sharing this moment of freedom with her. I sat her in front with me, and Edna took the back seat.

"Where are we going?" Vicky asked, putting on her seatbelt.

"If I told you, it wouldn't be a surprise now would it," I replied, tickling her stomach.

"You're going to love the surprise," Edna said, leaning forward from the back seat.

I took the Frozen CD out of the side compartment of my door, and asked her if she liked this CD. She said Frozen was her favourite movie, and after listening to her favourite song on repeat incessantly, all three of us knew the words, and we were doing a carpool karaoke, and must've looked like complete lunatics to our fellow road users, as we drove to Bloubergstrand. But I didn't care, it was all so worth it just to get one smile from Vicky. There was hardly any traffic, so we got to

Blouberg quite quickly, it was a really hot, but windy, so after buying us ice-creams on a cone, we found a nice spot on the beach and just sat there marvelling at the sea, the cool breeze on our face, and the gentle ebb and flow of the waves whispering in our ears.

"Uncle Gideon," Vicky said, tugging my right arm after we finished our ice creams. "I want to feel the ocean on my face. Can you please take me to the water?"

"Vicky, sweetheart," I replied, "I'd love to but I don't think that's a good idea because it might make you sicker."

"He's right sweetheart," Edna ran her fingers through Vicky's hair. "The cold water isn't going to do you any good."

"Uncle Gideon," Vicky took a deep breath, looked at Edna then turned towards me and said something that shattered my heart, and left me completely powerless. "Being sick has stolen a lot from me, I can't play outside like other kids, I can't go to school like other kids, I can't do anything like other kids, being sick has even taken my parents from me. I don't even know if I'm ever going to get better, nor do I know if I am ever going to get a chance to see the ocean again, please don't let my being sick steal the ocean from me too."

I looked at Edna, we both had tears in our eyes. I was doing my utmost to stay positive and ignore that her words sounded so much like a death wish, how could I refuse her?

"Vicky," I replied, holding out my right pinkie finger. "I will take you to the water, but you have to make me two promises, ok?"

"Yay," she smiled, "what are they?"

"When we go to the water, promise me you'll never let go of me."

"I promise!" She shouted, "what's the other one?"

"And..." I grabbed hold of her pinkie with my finger. "Promise me you'll never give up fighting."

Vicky looked into my eyes, and must've noticed that I wanted to cry because she leaned forward, gave me a hug and whispered in my ear, "I promise."

I took my jacket, socks and shoes off, rolled my pants up to my knees and took Vicky into my arms. The cold water cooled my skin as I stepped farther and farther into the tide. I held tightly onto Vicky, who had her tiny arms around my neck. Then I closed my eyes and said a little prayer: "Dear Lord Jesus, I don't know what you plans for Vicky are, but as I'm standing here with her in my arms, I'm begging you please not to take Vicky away from her parents... or me. Amen." She shrieked with delight as the waves gently crashed against my body, and drenched us both. I thought of the Bible story of when Jesus was baptized in the river Jordan, and I asked Jesus to baptize her too now in His Holy Fire. I just closed my eyes, and basked in the moment, expectant of having the Holy Spirit poured out over us.

"Gideon... Gideon..." I could feel the words deep in my heart. "Don't forget who I am, as I was with Gillian and with you, so will I be with Vicky. She is my child, as you all are."

It was the first time I had felt the presence of Christ so strongly since my time in heaven, and it left me with a sense of immense peace and gratitude. I always thought that having experienced heaven, would've given me a special connection to heaven. But it actually had the opposite effect, because of that experience, the limitations of my flesh had become all the more overwhelming and difficult to deal with at times. So I cherished this moment with Vicky and prayed that she could feel the peace too.

As the waters continued to envelope us with the tides, Vicky wiped the excess water from her face and her beaming smile warmed my heart.

"Are you ready to go back now?"

"Yes Uncle Gideon," she responded. "Thank you so much."

I walked back to the shore and covered Vicky with my jacket after Nurse Edna had thoroughly dried her with a face towel she had brought along.

"You're drenched!" Edna laughed.

"And it's the best feeling in the world," I replied.

We opened the picnic basket and enjoyed our seaside lunch before driving back home. Claire was on the verge of killing us when she found out what I had done, but calmed down immediately when she saw how happy Vicky was. She insisted that Edna monitor her closely.

"Please be more careful next time, we can't be taking unnecessary risks," she said, before taking a deep breath. "But thank you." She smiled.

Chapter Eighteen

2 Corinthians 1:10
He has delivered us from such a deadly peril, and he will deliver us again.
On him we have set our hope that he will continue to deliver us.

It had been two weeks since I had taken the test, and still no results, I was getting anxious but doing my utmost not to show it, especially around Vicky. We had been spending a lot of time together, she was the closest to a daughter that I ever had on earth, and I was enjoying every moment of my time with her, but always keeping my mother's words at the back of my mind: *"Gideon, please don't replace Gillian in your heart with this little girl, Vicky..."* I had been reading her bed time stories, playing with her in the playground during my lunch intervals, holding her during times when she was feeling sick and just talking to her about everything and nothing.

"Uncle Gideon," she said, as I tucked her into bed. "Are my parents ever going to come back?"

"Vicky, of course they are going to come back for you! Why would you even ask that?" I didn't say it, but I understood exactly why she asked the question. At least one of them should've been here with her, humans have this tendency to want to go out and save the world from disaster, while not noticing the fires raging at home.

"I don't know..." she sighed. "I just miss them I guess."

"Sweetheart," I replied hugging her, "your parents love you very much, and they are out there desperately searching for medicine to make you all better so that you can all go back to being the happy family that you always were."

"Uncle Gideon," she hugged me a little tighter as she rested her head on my shoulder. "If they don't come back, can I stay with you please?"

"Hey, hey," I pulled her back and gently caressed her cheek. "Your parents are going to come back for you because they love you more than you can ever imagine..."

"How do you know? You don't even know them." She shrugged.

"I know because like them, I had a daughter once too..." Speaking about Gillian now brought me peace and joy. "She was beautiful and amazing just like you, and if I could turn back time I would do what your parents are doing now... Anything and everything to save her."

"What happened to her?"

"Jesus needed her."

"Was she sick like me?"

"Her sickness was a little bit different to yours."

"Does he need me too?"

"Of course, he needs us all," I replied. "Some of us he needs here, and some of us he needs up there, in heaven," I pointed up to the sky. "Just trust him."

"What was your daughter's name?"

"Gillian..." My heart was longing to be with her now. "I think it's way past your bed time Missy."

"No it's not, you just want to stop talking," she giggled.

"You're much smarter than I look," I laughed and tucked her into bed. "Sweetheart, your parents are coming back for you, and until then, I will be here. Goodnight and sleep with God's angels."

"Thank you Uncle Gideon," I kissed her on the forehead, switched off her bedside lamp and left the room.

As I made my way to the reception area, I noticed that Claire wasn't at her desk, but left her laptop open, thinking she may have forgotten it I was going to shut it down for her and pack it away. But as I leaned forward to shut down her system, I noticed something that made my blood run cold. She had a document open on her screen, and the words at the top of the page read: *Dear friends and family, my time has come...*

"What are you doing at my PC?" Claire's voice sounded indignant as she entered the room.

"I thought you had forgotten it... So I was shutting..."

"How dare you touch my personal belongings..."

"I'm sorry..."

"Just get out!" She marched forward and snatched the laptop off her desk.

"I was just trying..."

"To what?" She snapped "To help?"

"Claire, I don't know what's wrong but..."

"Just get out please Gideon, go home," her voice was getting louder and more aggressive.

"Ok," I replied. "I'm sorry..." Without saying another word, I just walked out as she asked.

"I'm pretty sure that was a suicide note..." I said to myself in the car, head-butting my steering wheel. "I don't know how to help her."

"Do what I did for you," A familiar voice rose up from deep within me. *"Just listen to her."*

"Lord," I bowed my head in prayer, not shocked at his presence because I knew he was always with me as he had promised to be with his disciples until the end of time. But I was just in awe at how he always came to my aid, when I needed it most. "But she doesn't even want to see me?"

"You weren't planning on seeing me either," He laughed. "But I never gave up on you, so imitate my example and don't give up on her."

He left me with those words, and a renewed sense of hope, that although I may not always realize it or feel it, I need to hold onto my faith that he is always with me whenever I call on his name, and with Claire, I was going to have to call on him to help. I noticed her walking out, she had tears running down her face. I decided to follow her, I had no idea where she was going, but if I was right and that document was really a suicide note, she could be preparing to take her own life today, I couldn't let that happen. The roads were very quiet for a Friday night, the streetlights whizzed past my window as I put in all efforts to stay on her tail, without her realizing I was following her.

She was leaving Paarl, so I knew she wasn't going home. Not a good sign. I just kept following her at a safe distance. Somewhere between Paarl and the road that led to her unknown destination, she turned onto a gravel road, I waited a little while before turning so I could continue following her undetected. I dimmed my headlights and kept going, about three kilometres in, I noticed she parked her car next to a tree, so I stopped my car right there and continued on foot. Claire was crying and I saw she grabbed something out of the backseat of her car, then she sat underneath the tree and just looked out into the distance of the dark sky that stretched out above us. I walked slowly, so she wouldn't hear my footsteps...

"Why, Jason?" She said in between her sobbing. "You were all I had for the longest time... And just like everyone else, you left."

"Jesus, help me do this," I whispered to myself as I edged a little closer to her.

"Why here?" I spoke up once I was within footsteps of her.

"What..." she wiped her face. "Why are you following me!?"

"Because when I was where you are, I wish someone had followed me," I said. "The road to hell has no detours Claire, there's still time for you to turn around."

"Yeah, well I'm not sure I want to turn around..." she replied. "Don't think I have any reason to."

"I didn't think I had any reasons to turn around either," I sat down next to her. "And yet here I am, underneath the black sky sitting with you. Why here?"

"What do you mean?"

"We always return to the place where our pain started and life as we knew it ended," I replied. "I guess it just makes the ending more poetic right? To die physically where you had died spiritually... A last ditch effort at making life the beautiful work of art we always hoped it would've been."

Claire stared at me for a moment, part of her face shining in the moonlight. Her tear-stained cheeks looked like cracked glass. She grabbed her phone, got up and walked over to the tree, switching on the flashlight, she shone it onto the tree trunk: "J 4 C" was engraved into the eternity sign in big letters.

"His name is Jason," I said, "I know it's the mother of all clichés but I caught him red-handed in bed with his bass guitarist, he's a musician." She started to cry again. "I grew up in an orphanage, my whole life it was me against the world until I met Jason..."

"I'm sorry Jason put you right back in the orphanage where you believed you weren't good enough for anyone," I replied. I got up and gave her a hug, as she washed her pain away with tears.

"So what's your story?" Claire said, several minutes later after composing herself.

We sat down under the tree and I told her everything from being married, to losing my daughter, to the suicide attempt and how I went to heaven and met Jesus, who literally saved me from hell.

"I can't say I'm totally fine now," I said, "I'm still human, still in the same body, still haunted by the same dreams, broken by the same memories... But at least now I have renewed hope. When I lose sense of who I am here, I remember where I'm headed and who I've been created to be and that helps me look up for the light of Jesus who leads us all out of darkness if we let him."

"I'm sorry for your losses," Claire said, "Now I understand why you're so connected to Vicky."

"Thank you," I replied, "sometimes I try and keep my distance because I know that she's not mine, but I can't help it. She reminds me so much of Gillian, and the way I see it, Jesus put her on my path so I can be there for her while her parents are away... the truth is she's the one who's healing me every day."

"Wait here..." I noticed that what she had taken out of her backseat was a rope. So I grabbed it on my way back to my car, where I remembered I had a Bible in the cubby hole that I wanted to give her.

"What's this?"

"It's a Bible," I said, putting it on her lap. "Can I pray for you?"

"Thank you," she replied. "I don't know about the prayers..."

"All you have to do is close your eyes and just picture your pain... I will pray for you."

She agreed, we held hands and I just prayed for her from the heart, knowing all too well what it feels like to not want to die but also not have the energy to live either. In many ways Claire reminded me of who I was and where I was at her age. We all have this idea of how our lives are going to be and exactly how the world is going to turn by the time we're twenty-five, but then reality hits us in a massive way and before we know it, we're in our thirties wondering what happened to the last decade of our lives. If I could spare Claire that confusion and regret of lost time, then I was going to do everything I could for her.

"Thank you..." She said.

"Open the Bible right now, just anywhere," I prompted her.

"2 Corinthians 1:10," She said.

"Before it was Jason and Claire," I said, walking over to the tree where she showed me the engraving of her initials. "Now let it be Jesus and Claire, because trust me, in times when you have no one else. He will be there, leading you out of the darkness."

"Thank you Gideon," she gave me another hug. "Please don't tell anyone about this."

"I won't have to," I replied, "because once you've experienced Jesus's light leading you out of the darkness. You'll tell everyone about this yourself."

Chapter Nineteen

Psalm 23

The Lord is my shepherd, I lack nothing. He makes me lie down in green pastures, he leads me beside quiet waters, he refreshes my soul. He guides me along the right paths for his name's sake. Even though I walk through the darkest valley, I will fear no evil, for you are with me, your rod and my staff, they comfort me. You prepare a table for me in the presence of my enemies. You anoint my head with oil, my cup overflows, surely your goodness and love will follow me all the days of my life, and I will dwell in the house of the Lord forever.

"The results arrived from the lab," Claire said, holding up the envelope.

"Open it!"

Claire opened it and upon reading I could see the tears welling up in her eyes. "You're a match."

"Thank you Lord," I dropped to my knees and praised God, after we shouted for joy together.

"I'm going to phone her parents," Claire said.

"Can we tell Vicky?"

"I'll give you the honours," Claire smiled.

"Awesome," Claire stopped me just as I was about to rush off.

"You're an amazing guy Gideon," Claire said. "You're like the big brother I never had... thank you."

"Thanks Sis," I replied, winking at her. "Since we've adopted each other as siblings, I want you to know that any potential future boyfriends will need to get my approval, ok?"

"Shut up." Claire laughed.

"You're an amazing young woman Claire, and sooner or later God is going to open some very special guy's eyes to see you and value you the way he does, and you will just know. Until then, just keep doing your best and allow him to do the rest."

We looked at each other for a moment, somewhere deep down I had the feeling that if I was younger or she was older, we'd be right for each other. But I didn't have romantic feelings for her, just a deep sense of wanting her to be ok. I was far from being an angel, but I likened what I felt for Claire to what our guardian angels must feel for us, doing everything according to God's will to make sure we recognize in ourselves that which God created us to be.

"Well," I said, "going to tell Vicky the good news."

As I crossed the garden and play area to Vicky's room, I couldn't contain my excitement. The last time I was this excited was when Lillian told me she was pregnant. Vicky wasn't my child, but I was as happy and honoured to be her donor as if I was her own father. I couldn't stop thanking Jesus for allowing me to be the instrument in his hand to heal her.

"Vicky," I said, knocking on her door. There was no response. "Vicky?" I knocked again.

I panicked and all of a sudden my heart was getting ready to rip through my chest, as I opened her door and saw her lying unconscious on the floor next to her bed in a pile of her own sick. Her face was as pale as a ghost, and she was burning up in fever.

"Somebody help!" I shouted, cradling her in my arms and rushing out of the room to the bathrooms.

"What happened?" Nurse Edna rushed over.

"I don't know, I went to her room and found her lying on the ground like this," I replied, "run a bath for her, she's burning up, we need to break her fever."

"What happened!?" Claire shouted arriving on the scene.

"I found her passed out in her room, she's burning up with fever," I replied. "Call her Doctor now."

"On it," Claire rushed out.

"Come on baby," I said, taking off her pyjama top and pants off and gently lowering her into the bath tub while running the cool water over her head. "Hang on... we're so close."

"The Doctor said we better take her to the hospital," Claire returned. "I've called an ambulance because they will get her there faster than what we can."

"Great," I replied. "Thanks."

"Vicky," I could see her regaining consciousness and groaning in pain. "Thank God," I whispered.

"It's ok," I said, cradling her as she cried onto my shoulder. "I got you angel."

"Daddy, I'm sick."

"I know sweetheart," I whispered, "but Claire has phoned the doctor and the ambulance is going to come get you so that you can feel all better, ok?" I didn't bother correcting her. She needed a dad, and in that moment, I needed a daughter, so we were exactly what we needed to be for each other.

"Will you come with me?"

"Of course," I said. "Remember I promised to be here for you until your parents come back. I'm not going anywhere." The ambulance arrived, and within minutes after hooking her up to an IV, we were ready to go.

"Gideon, I'll meet you there," Claire said, "she's going to be ok." She held my hands.

"I hope so."

The paramedic closed the door behind us and proceeded to pull away from the clinic. With the sirens blaring above my head, a thousand scenarios raced through my mind as I watched Vicky on the edges of consciousness, her tiny body lying on that stretcher next to me.

My heart was heavy, and my stomach was in knots; if she had to die now, knowing that I was a suitable donor is something that I don't think I would ever get over. It would be like losing Gillian all over again, I don't think I could survive that. Before long we were at Paarl Mediclinic, and as they wheeled her through to the emergency ward, all I could do was wait, pacing back and forth in the waiting area for what felt like an eternity.

"Gideon," Claire arrived with coffee. "I understand you concern, but no amount of worry is going to help her. Try drink some coffee at least, and take a breather."

"Thanks," I accepted her coffee.

Claire got up the minute she noticed Vicky's doctor emerging from the ward with a facial expression that I just couldn't quite fathom. My stomach knotted up again.

"Dr Lee," Claire said, "please tell me she's ok?"

"How is she?" I followed up in haste.

"Is this man her father?"

"No Dr," Claire responded. "He works at the care centre with me. He's like her guardian."

"Gideon Daniels," I said, pulling out the envelope with the lab results from my pocket. "I'm a match for her bone marrow transplant. I'm willing to do it today."

"Thank you Mr Daniels," He took the letter from me. "Her white blood cell count is very low, and that is not a good sign given her condition, but I don't want to give a diagnosis until we've conducted all the tests. We can't treat her until we get that fever back to normal and stabilized her, so the next 12 hours will be crucial. But yes, if we stabilize her, then we can proceed with the surgery as early as tomorrow morning. You will need to stay the night though to get prepped for surgery Mr Daniels."

"That's fine," I said, "will go home and get ready and be back within the hour." All the way home and back, I thought about all the different things I could've done or should've done in order to make sure that Vicky was ok and no in her current predicament. I felt like I had failed her... Just like I failed Lillian... And Gillian.

"Thank you," he smiled. "Claire, I will keep you posted."

"Thank you Doctor Lee."

GETTING DRESSED INTO the hospital attire brought back less than pleasant memories of my brushes with hospitals; from the time they removed my tonsils as a little kid, to the broken hip and suicide attempt as an adult, I haven't got pleasant memories of hospitals, which is ironic, since hospitals are there to save people's lives. But luckily this time around, my hospital stay was for a good cause, and not due to some unfortunate accident. This did nothing to diminish the discomfort of the cotton robes and smell of antiseptics. The nurse on duty introduced herself as Fatima to me, and we struck up a conversation because I was the only healthy patient in her observation ward.

"Is Victoria your daughter?" She asked, filling in my chart after checking my blood pressure.

"No," I replied, "she's just a very special girl who came into my life by God's grace."

"I'm assuming you're a Christian?" She asked.

"You assume correct," I smiled, "and what about you?"

"I'm Hindu," she replied.

"I'm not too familiar with your faith," I said, "but I don't like to judge anyone. You clearly have a good heart, or else you wouldn't be here, helping people and playing a part in saving people's lives."

"Thank you," she said, straightening my pillows and making sure I was comfortable. "I'm not here to judge anyone either, but I have to admit that Christianity does make me curious. With all due respect, I think Christianity takes man's capacity for evil far too lightly... As a

Hindu, I believe in karma, everything we do has consequences. This 'forgive and forget' policy of Christianity is hard for me to understand, much less accept."

"I understand what you mean," I replied with a hearty laugh. "But we believe Jesus died for our sins and bore the consequences of them on our behalf. It's not that we make light of evil, our actions always have consequences. But because Jesus died in our place, and put to death the consequences of sin, through Him we have the chance to be redeemed, so we don't have to face the consequences of the sin on our souls, if we choose to change our ways and follow Him."

"Thanks for the chat Mr Daniels," Fatima responded, "you're a good man for giving a child a chance at a new life. That's good enough for me."

"Thank you," I said. "How is Victoria?"

"Dr Lee hasn't given us a report back, but as they say, no news is good news," she put my file back in the shelf at my bedside. "I will come and check in on you later."

"Thank you, may I go for a walk?"

"Sure, just don't go outside please."

I walked around the hospital, observing the patients in each ward; some were happy, surrounded by family, the plans for their future, alive in their smiles. Others were sad, no doubt knowing that this would be the last corner they would turn on their journey, the sadness of the prolonged goodbye written on their faces. Then there were those who were completely alone, they all had the most distant look in their eyes, like they had died years before they arrived at this current moment. Hospitals were just museums for human life. I got to the cafeteria and ordered a coffee, after explaining that I was in observation because I was going in for a bone marrow transplant.

I was thinking about all the patients I had just come across, each one a culmination of choices that led up to the very moment they were living in. I started thinking about the culmination of my choices and what influenced them; imaging what my life would've looked like if I had made different choices. If I hadn't married Lillian, I probably would've focused on my career, become the person I had always dreamed of becoming before I met Lillian. But then again, if I had never met Lillian, I never would've had Gillian. People always talk about balance, but when it comes to heartbreak, no amount of balance fixes broken.

"Life is too short to be miserable..." I whispered to myself, taking another sip of my latte.

"And eternity is too long for us to spend our time worrying about something that's going to end eventually," a man said, walking by my table. "Mind if I sit?"

"Go ahead," I gestured for him to take the seat opposite me.

"Thanks," he got comfortable. "I'm on a lunch break."

"You a nurse?" I asked.

"Nope," he replied. "Cleaning staff."

"Why did you remind me about eternity?"

"I've watched people in here grappling with regrets, they all wished for the same thing, more time... what do you think they want more time for?"

"I guess to try and make amends?" I said.

"Gideon," he said. "Not everything that's broken needs to be fixed, sometimes we take the pieces, move on and build something else. 95% of the people wish they had more time not so much because they want to make amends, but rather because they realize they've spent their entire lives trying to be people they were never created to be. Now at the moment of truth, when they realize they are going to meet their maker and have to answer for why they wasted their time being who they believed they should be, instead of who they were created to be, they are filled with regret." He reached out and grabbed my hand. "If you're alive it's because God is giving you another chance. Don't waste your rehearsal time preparing for a part you were never called to play, because once production starts there's no turning back."

We sat there and looked at each other for a moment, I had this sudden deep sensation that I knew him from somewhere. He stood up and walked away, when I remembered something...

"Hey," I said, "How did you know my name?"

"Let's just say I've been watching you from afar," he smiled, and I caught a glimpse of his nametag: Gabriel.

Chapter Twenty

John 14:1-4
*"Let not your hearts be troubled. Believe in God; believe
also, in me. In my Father's house are many rooms. If it were not so,
would I have told you that I go to prepare a place for you? And if I
go and prepare a place for you, I will come again and will take you
to myself, that where I am you may be also. And you know the way
to where I am going."*

In all the drama of the day, I completely forgot to call my mom, clearly she phoned to check up on me at work, and Claire filled her in. So after making a grand entrance to the hospital, and lecturing me for not keeping her informed; she kept asking me and everyone else who would care to listen if I was okay, and to make sure I wasn't dying of some disease.

"Dr Lee," Claire said.

"Dr Lee!" My mother rushed to his side, "I'm Gideon's mother, is he okay? Does he have some disease that he hasn't told me about? Is he going to die?"

"Mrs Daniels," Dr Lee smiled, "from what I've seen so far... your son is going to outlive us all."

"Thank God!" She shouted.

"I have good news," Dr Lee said, "Victoria's fever has broken, she's stable and we can do the transplant tomorrow. Gideon, your surgery is scheduled for tomorrow morning at 9am. Remember, no food after 8 pm."

"Of course, thank you Dr."

He left us, and everyone wished me luck. My mom was telling me about how she phoned all our family to prepare them for the worst, so she was going to have to go back home and phone them again to calm the widespread panic she caused.

"I love you mom," I said and kissed her on the forehead before she left.

"The moment of truth Mister," Claire said, "I went to see Vicky earlier, she's very weak, but stable and she said she misses you."

"Tell her I miss her more."

"I will," she smiled. "Are you afraid?"

"At the risk of not qualifying to be your protective big brother," I replied. "Yes, I'm terrified."

"You'll be ok," she said, grabbing my hand. "I will be right here, when you get back. I promise."

"Any chance you could be here with a beer when I get back?" I joked, "I might need it."

"I will try my best," she laughed.

"You're going to be fine," she said, "I will be praying for you."

I WAS WHEELED INTO theatre, it wasn't the first surgery I had done, but no matter how many times a person goes under the knife, I don't think anyone gets comfortable with the idea of having someone cut into their body. God's love has been compared to a fire, so within the context of that comparison, if God's love was a fire, then death might be the confines of an operating theatre. It was freezing cold in there, and as I looked around at all the machines and surgical utensils, I felt powerless on that table. One of the nurses covered me with a blanket, and I recognized Dr Lee's voice from behind the many masked faces hovering above me.

"Mr Daniels," he said, "we're going to administer the anaesthetic and I want you to start counting backwards from 100 please?" His eyes wrinkled as I noticed him smiling from behind his surgical mask.

"99...98...97..." I could feel my head spin and the room faded to black.

Thanks to my previous encounter with Jesus, I knew I wasn't in heaven, but judging from my surroundings, I was somewhere in between heaven and earth. I was sitting on a cloud, surrounded by the vast blue expanse of an endless summer sky, I felt no pain or anxiety, but no profound joy either, just a sense of peace and expectant hope. The same feeling I had when I received the lab results to say I was a match for Victoria's bone marrow transplant.

"Jesus?" I called out, wondering if He would come to see me.

A man dressed in white robes and large wings came gliding towards me and stopped beside me on a separate cloud. We had met before, it was the angel Gabriel.

"Gabriel," I smiled.

"Shalom Gideon," he responded.

"Where is Jesus?"

"Your time to meet him again has not arrived," he replied. "He has sent me to give you another message. He wants me to remind you to not forget him, no matter how dark the world gets, do not lose sight of his light."

"I'm not sure what he wants me to do," I said, "was it just to save Victoria? Is he going to take me now so I can be with Gillian?"

"Only Abba knows what plans He has for your time on earth," Gabriel replied. "Your task, like every other one of His children is simply to follow Him and trust Him with as much faith as your heart can muster... do your best, and allow Him to do the rest."

"Were you the man I saw in the cafeteria today?"

But he did not answer me and slowly retreated back into the clouds, leaving me alone to ponder his words. I didn't know what to make of this, but I had had enough experiences with Jesus to know that He never overwhelms us with His plans because He knows we are not capable of handling it. So even with this, as Gabriel said, my only duty was to keep following and trusting Him with as much faith as my heart could muster. I could feel my senses returning to my body as I slowly woke up from the anaesthetic, I was really groggy and had a dull pain in my right hip. I was back in the ward, and I recognized Claire and my mom standing side by side, mom was clutching onto her rosary beads and praying audibly. There was a third person in the room, an unfamiliar face.

"Hey champion," Claire said, "how are you feeling?"

"Great..." My voice sounded like a rusty toolbox.

"Gideon sweetheart," My mom leaned forward and spoke loudly to make sure I hadn't gone deaf.

"Hello Mom," I smiled.

"Oh thank the Lord, He recognizes me," she said.

"This is Mr Peter Langdon," Claire said, beckoning the stranger to come forward. "Vicky's father."

"Oh, pleased to meet you Mr Langdon," I replied.

"Please call me Peter," he smiled. "The pleasure is all mine, thank you for saving my daughter's life Gideon, I will be forever indebted to you."

"Victoria's a very special girl Peter," I replied. "I'm just happy and honoured to be the instrument that God chose to heal her."

"Thank you," he smiled. "Well, I will let you rest. My wife couldn't make it and we are still settling in, unfortunately I have some other business to attend to, so I won't be joining her later, but she will be here. Going to check on Vicky before I go, rest well Gideon."

"Please give her my best." He nodded in agreement before leaving the room.

"He's an atheist," Claire whispered, noticing how I picked up on his unsettling exit.

"I can't believe it," I replied and we had a good laugh, despite how ravaging the after effects of the anaesthetic continued to be.

True to form, my mother brought a banquet of food in her bag and I had to promise her I would eat it before they discharge me, so she wouldn't spoon-feed me. We chatted about the latest developments in the current soapie she was following. Slowly but surely, I regained my strength, and all I could think about now was how Vicky was doing. They were giving her the bone-marrow and promised that I would be able to see her first thing in the morning. My mom remembered that she had left the stove on and promised to come back tomorrow morning with a hearty breakfast and guaranteed that she would phone me tonight, because she didn't want to miss the latest episode of her soapie. I told her it would be absolutely fine and she could leave with my blessing.

"Your mom is such a character," Claire laughed.

"Like a cartoon character right?" I said, "I completely agree."

"Don't be mean," Claire laughed.

"She's my mom, no matter what, I will always love her."

"Well, I've got to run too," she got up and kissed my forehead. "Without you there, things have been hectic, so I got to be there. Sorry about the beer but I drank it on the way here."

"Now you going to owe me two," I smiled. "See you later."

I had no idea how much time had gone by, but one of the worst things about hospital was the solitude. My grandmother used to say that the best place to know who your friends are is when you are in hospital, besides the nurses who were getting paid to check up on me at regular intervals, I was happy to count Claire as one of my friends. I grabbed the remote, and started flipping through the channels, I settled on 7de Laan to keep me company, I had taken a painkiller and started to dose off when I suddenly heard a familiar voice from a distant past...

"Hello, Gideon..."

"Lillian!?" My heart jolted within my chest and my stomach turned. Despite the odd extra wrinkle on her face, she was still just as beautiful as the day I had last seen her. "What the hell are you doing here!?"

"I'm here..."

"You ruined my life a decade ago, and disappeared," I was fuming. "Without so much as an explanation and now you just waltz back into my life?" My voice was getting louder. I could see the nurses getting closer. "What could you possibly want from me now!?"

"Gideon!" She shouted. "I'm Victoria's mother!"

"What!?" I gasped after an eternity of awkward silence.

"That's right Gideon," she was crying now. "Of all the people God could've chosen to be the bone marrow donor for my daughter, he chose my ex-husband.... Can you believe it? So trust me Gideon, this is equally uncomfortable for me!?"

"Is everything ok here?" The nurse approached us.

"Everything is fine," I said, "I just found out Victoria's mom is my ex-wife that's all."

"I understand how complicated this might be for you both, but I'm going to have to ask you to keep your voices down and be civilized, there are other patients in this hospital who need to rest, as do you Mr Daniels."

"I'm sorry," Lillian said.

"Right," I said, "I'm sorry."

"God's got some sense of humour right?" Lillian said, after I took some time to process the cataclysmic storm that had hit me.

"So that's why you couldn't join Peter earlier," I said, "you already knew it was me."

"I've known since the beginning," she said, "Claire sent us pictures of you and Vicky together. So I've had time to process all of this.

"I'm assuming Mr Langdon doesn't know?"

"I'm still struggling to comprehend it myself, how can I make him understand?"

"Of course," I replied. "We both know explanations have never been your forte."

"You're pretty judgemental for someone who has apparently found God," she snapped.

"Oh, well excuse me if the reappearance of my ex-wife who cheated on me and disappeared a decade ago causes me to be perfectly human and disturbs you," I said, "so what happened with you and your boss? Or is it because Mr Langdon is richer than him?"

"I deserve that," she said. "We called it quits after six months, he didn't want to leave his wife for me." She sat down in the chair next to my bed and looked into my eyes. "Gideon, I was a mess after losing Gillian, we both were... We were both painful reminders to each other of the life we once had. I was young and naïve, my dreams were just too big for the box we had fit our life together into and that isn't your fault. I know I am ten years too late, but Gideon..." she grabbed my hand and I just couldn't pull it away from her. "I am really and truly sorry for hurting you." Her eyes brimmed with tears.

The memories of our life together hit me like a flood. "Do you know how many sleepless nights I had, wondering in what ways and why I just wasn't good enough for you? I fell apart and because of you there are parts of me that I will never get back."

"Gideon, I know," she closed her eyes. "You're an amazing guy, much better than I ever deserved. There's nothing I can do that will justify my actions or take your pain away, I can't change the past, all I can do is say I am sorry and I'm not even expecting you to forgive me. But please know that I am sorry with all my heart and forever grateful that you saved me daughter's life. I will be forever indebted to you for that."

"How is she?"

"She's stable," Lillian's eyes became distant. "But we'll have to wait and see now."

"It's truly ironic," I said, "we lost Gillian, now I'm the one who was chosen to save the daughter you had with another man."

"Claire told me how much Victoria loves you, and I could see it's true by all the pictures she had sent me," Lillian said, "thank you for being there for her, when we couldn't be. You will always be a part of her life. I will make sure of it."

"You can't use your daughter to make amends for what you did to me," I snapped.

"But I can try..." she leaned forward, slipped an ipod into my hands with earphones and got ready to leave. "Goodbye Gideon, thank you for saving Vicky, I will never be able to repay you, but I will spend my life trying."

SHE WALKED OUT OF THE ward, leaving only the familiar smell of her perfume in the ward to remind me of our happy memories. There was a note attached to the ipod that read: *"Music speaks where words fail."-Victor Hugo.* There was only one song on the ipod... *"I don't know you anymore"* by Savage Garden; and just like that, with tears streaming down my face, she left me in pieces... again.

Chapter Twenty-One

Romans 8:28
And we know that all things God works for the good of those who love
Him, who have been called according to His purpose.

"Uncle Gideon!" Vicky was still very pale, but at least her energy levels were much better.

"Sweetheart, how I missed you," I hugged her like the whole world depended on it.

We chatted over ice cream, and I confess that I was starting to sound as overbearing as my mother at questioning her about how she was feeling. She assured me with a good number of rolling eyes how fine she felt.

"So did you meet my mom and dad?"

"Yes I sure did," I said, "are you happy they are back?"

"Yes!" She raised her arms. "They are special, but so are you."

"Aww thank you Vicky," I replied, "but none of us are as special as you."

"Alright sweetheart," I got up, "I'm going to let you rest."

"Uncle Gideon," she called out to me. "I love you."

"I love you too sweetheart," I kissed her on the forehead and let her rest.

FIVE WEEKS LATER...

"Ashes to ashes," the priest said, "dust to dust..."

"How are you holding up?" Claire came up behind me and grabbed my arm.

"As well as can be expected," I replied, holding her hand.

"She's watching over you," she said.

"I know..." I replied. "Doesn't make it any easier though, I'm just tired of losing everything and everyone I give my heart to."

"I'm sorry bro," she said. "I know your life has been a complete fiasco, what with her mom being your ex-wife and all that, but Romans 8:28, something good has come out of all this, even if you don't see it right now."

"Look at you quoting scripture to me," I smiled. "I'm proud of you."

"Thank you," she smiled. "By the way, I've met someone..."

"Oh really?" I replied. "I hope he's not a musician?"

"Actually..."

"Oh no..." I sighed. "Old habits die hard."

"His name is Tristan," she took out her phone and showed me a picture of a young man who was clean cut, but had a modern hairstyle, as if he belonged in a boy band. "He teaches music at the college in town and plays in his church choir."

"At least he doesn't have his own band," I smiled.

"Oh stop it," she punched my shoulder.

"So, when do I get to meet him, so I can give him my stamp of approval?"

"I will make a plan soon," she said and looked at her watch. "Oh goodness, I've got to run, are you sure you're going to be ok?"

"Yes," I replied. "I will see you later."

"Hey Gideon," she said, looking me in the eyes. "I know you have this tendency of saving people from the ocean to distract yourself from the fact that you're drowning, but don't get lost out there," she kissed me on the cheek. "You're my superhero. I love you buddy."

"I love you too Sis," her words were like a soothing balm to my aching soul.

Victoria didn't make it. The cancer metastasized to her liver, lungs and pancreas. There was nothing more the doctors could do, and as they lowered the casket into the ground, a chunk of my heart went with it, piece by piece, tear by tear. There were so many people, most of them I didn't recognize, I didn't want people to know I was there, so I disguised myself behind a black trench coat, fedora and sunglasses. All I could think about were the times Vicky and I spent together; her warm smile, the way her eyes would close when she let out a hearty laugh and the way her head would fit perfectly in my arms as I cradled her to sleep. I was broken, but if I had to do it all again, I wouldn't change a thing, because it was all worth it in the end.

As people dispersed from the funeral home, I took the opportunity to go visit Gillian's grave. When the world fades like the sun slowly gives way to darkness, that's when we're left with nothing but the shadows of what we imagined our life to be. I was completely confused and didn't know what to make of my life right now, I had lost Gillian and was convinced that God's way of restoring me was by bringing Vicky into my life. Now she was gone too, and I was just so confused and lost all over again, without any clue of what I was going to do with the rest of my life. But if there was one thing I have learned lately is that when things in this life are bringing us to our knees and spinning beyond our control, then the only thing left for us to do is to pray, because prayer builds a spiritual bridge between us and God. So after looking one last time at Gillian's photograph, I kneeled down, put my hands together and closed my eyes in prayer.

"Gideon..." I turned around and saw Lillian and Peter behind me, arm in arm, visibly and understandably distraught.

"My condolences..." I said, getting up to face them.

"I know you're hurting just as much as we are," Peter said, "I just want to say thank you for all you did for her," he said fighting back tears. "You were there for her when I couldn't be, and I will always be grateful to you for that."

"If I had to do it all over again, I wouldn't change a thing," I replied. "Vicky was a very special girl, she reminded me of someone I lost a long time ago."

"Your daughter with Lillian," Peter replied.

"You told him?" I looked at Lillian, she just nodded in agreement without saying a word.

"I was an atheist my entire life Gideon," Peter said, "I'm committed to facts and coherent explanations. For me seeing has always been believing; but then with Vicky, I was suddenly confronted with a scenario that no amount of facts or coherency could explain. My daughter got terminally ill, and despite all my resources I couldn't find a match for her. Then you came along as if you had fallen out of the sky, a complete stranger and you were a match! Then from a complete stranger I came to learn that you had loved the love of my life before me," he put his arm around Lillian and held her tightly to himself, "and you had also felt what I am feeling now, the loss of your little girl. I'm sorry for your loss too. I know your pain now. And because of all this, I had no choice but to conclude that beyond that sky," he pointed to the sky above us, "is someone controlling all of this. God truly works in mysterious ways Gideon... You didn't just save Vicky when you donated your bone marrow... and I will be forever grateful for that." He hugged me.

"Gideon..." Lillian came forward and gave me a hug. "I'm so sorry... I guess I don't deserve to be a mother, or is God punishing me for hurting you."

"Lillian," I held her hands. "God doesn't punish us; we punish ourselves by removing ourselves from His presence. I blamed myself for losing you and Gillian for years, but God in His own way showed me that He loved me unconditionally, and no amount of failure was going to change that. He feels the same way about you... Just give Him a chance to show you. Gillian and Vicky are looking at us right now and smiling, because despite how we may have hurt each other, they've brought us together and showed us how alike we actually are. We lost each other because we let our pain get in the way of what we had, don't make the same mistake with Peter, he clearly loves you and is going to be there for you in ways that I probably couldn't be. Be there for him too." I was suddenly reminded of what Gillian said to me when I saw her in heaven, about how much she loved her Mother. How could I not forgive someone who has a part of themselves in Gillian whom I loved with all my heart? "We didn't get a chance to look after Gillian and Vicky, but they will always be looking after us from afar. You lost your daughters but you've gained Peter... and my forgiveness." I kissed her on the cheek.

"Thank you Gideon," she smiled and went back to Peter's side.

It was a bitter-sweet moment for me, as I watched Lillian walk away with Peter. But for the first time in my life, I made peace with it. I saw the anguish and guilt in her eyes, it mirrored my own. Losing Gillian and Vicky showed me how underneath all our differences, we were all the same. Lillian had acknowledged her mistake, and I remember standing before Jesus acknowledging all my mistakes too. I had to forgive her, the same way I was forgiven... It was the only way to set myself free of the pain of the moment when my world with her had come crashing down. I closed my eyes, raised my arms and just thanked God for the freedom. When I opened my eyes, I saw a vision of Jesus in the sky, He was standing with Gillian in one arm and Vicky in the other, they were smiling and waving at me.

I hadn't seen Vicky's hair because she was bald from the chemo when I met her, but there she was, with long golden hair. Jesus didn't have to say a word... His gaze and smile told me everything I needed to know, it's as if He was saying to me: *"In the same way my pain saved you, by giving me the pain they caused you, I was able to show them how my pain saved them too. You may not be profoundly happy right now, but keep going and know I will not forsake you, your treasures are safe in my arms, waiting for when I call you back home, where you will be for all eternity."*

I walked away with the confidence that Jesus's light is shining on me like the sun, and even in darkness, His light brings me hope and will always lead me home, where my heart is... in His arms.

<u>The End.</u>

Afterword

John 8:12
I am the light of the world, whoever walks with me will not walk in darkness.

Dear readers,

Along this path of life that I have stumbled through, I have learned that beyond the superficial differences and idiosyncrasies that separate us from one another, we are no different to each other. We all have the same wants, needs and whether we're aware of it or not, we all have a deep-rooted spiritual hunger that needs to be fulfilled. David wrote in Psalm 63, that his soul thirsted for the Lord, and his flesh yearned for him. This is a thirst and a yearning that we can all relate to.

The 55th chapter of the book of Isaiah in the NIV is titled *"an invitation to the thirsty"*. In John's gospel, chapter 4, Jesus provides an answer to this human longing and declares that whoever drinks of the water that he provides will never thirst again. Amen!

In this my first foray into the daunting genre of Christian fiction, I was hoping to illustrate that an encounter with Christ doesn't mean we can suddenly sit back because we've become invincible. An encounter with Christ is life changing, just like every single person in the Bible who encountered Christ, it's impossible for us to remain the same. But that encounter doesn't negate us from our responsibility to take the necessary steps that will change our lives. As a writer and someone who loves a profound quote, I am reminded of this one by Pablo Picasso, the great Spanish artist: *"Inspiration exists, but it must find you working."* In that same vein, Christ will change your life, but when he comes, he must find you repenting and surrendering. The protagonist in my book, Gideon, was blessed to have had an encounter with Christ that saved him from eternal damnation, but the minute he returned to his earthly body, he became susceptible to the same weaknesses and whims he had before he encountered Christ. He was plagued by the same painful memories, and struggled to overcome the events from his past that had conditioned him into the person he was. But the only difference after his encounter with Christ, was that now he had Jesus as his refuge and strength in times of need. So his strength may have failed at times, just like before, but his hope never did, and his hope in Christ became like an anchor for him, keeping him grounded and moving forward as he should. I hope this book helps you find the everlasting hope that each one of us have in Jesus Christ. He came to give each one of us hope of an abundant life when he gave up his life for us on the cross, in our place. We cannot be Jesus, we can only follow the example he left us. That is why we need his strength to fulfil the purpose for which he created us (Philippians 4:13).

In our own strength alone, we will fail, because we all fall short of His glory (Romans 3:23), but with Jesus's strength in us, as we strive to abide in him so that he may abide in us (John 15:4), we can fulfil all the work God has prepared for us in advance to do, because we are God's handiwork, created in Christ Jesus (Ephesians 2:10). I leave you with a quote by Saint Frances of Assisi: *"All the darkness in the world, cannot extinguish the light of a single candle."* No matter how dark the world gets, my prayer for you is that you may find the light of Christ, that will lead you and keep you out of darkness, as you strive to walk in it (John 8:12). In Jesus Name. Amen.

Shalom in Christ.

About the Author

My name is Marcio Goncalves, born in Johannesburg, South Africa on the 15th of May 1984 to Portuguese parents and currently ives in Cape Town. Lover of art, beer, chocolate and Jesus Christ. (Not in that order) Non-lover of arrogance and everything that stems from it, music not made from actual instruments and pineapple.(In that order).

Lover of a good quote too, below are three of my favourites, that in some way or form shape who I am, while going through the inevitable fluctuations of life in the never ending fight with gravity:

"Be yourself because everyone else is already taken."-Oscar Wilde.

" For I know the plans I have for you," declares the Lord, "plans to prosper you and not to harm you, plans to give you hope and a future. Then you will call on me and come and pray to me, and I will listen to you. You will seek me and find me when you seek me with all your heart."-God. Jeremiah 29:11-13. The bible.

"Simplicity is the ultimate sophistication." - Leonardo Da Vinci.

Read more at marciogonwriting.blogspot.com.